Euphemia and the Unexpected Enchantment

THE FENTONS BOOK 3 NEW EDITION

ALICIA CAMERON

Copyright © 2019 by Alicia Cameron

All rights reserved.

No portion of this book may be reproduced in any form without written permission from the publisher or author, except as permitted by U.S. copyright law.

Contents

1. Prologue — 1
2. A Bear Bursts In — 3
3. Tending the Sick — 18
4. A Tour of the Gardens — 24
5. Friends Reunited — 36
6. Another Garden Encounter — 52
7. Epilogue — 65
8. Eloise and the Gift of Enthusiasm — 68
9. Eva and the Stolen Kisses — 88
10. Annis and the Grand Plan — 135
11. Esther and the Impulsive Proposal — 160

Also By Alicia Cameron — 187

12. A Sample Chapter of Honoria and the Family Obligation: The Fentons Book 1 — 193

13. A Sample Chapter of Georgette and the Unrequited   201
    Love: The Sisters of Castle Fortune 1

Afterword   209

CHAPTER ONE

Prologue

Lady Aurora Fenton was in her bed, involved in taking little snippets from her breakfast tray, whilst reading some letters that had arrived for her. She was a beauty of indeterminate age, swathed in a frothy lace concoction (surely from Paris) and known as one of the most fashionable ladies in London. Her days as the keeper of a house of chance had accustomed her to late hours, and she found it hard to dress before 11 of the clock. Her husband, a trim elegant figure, in a fashionable dark suit but with an added gold silk waistcoat which might have belonged to another age, re-entered her chamber, and perched on the bed to steal from her coffee cup and breakfast dainties. Since he had left her chamber a mere hour ago, she had, of course, made some subtle changes to her appearance. Her hair, though still falling on her shoulders in the same torrent that he had so recently let fall through his fingers, had been dressed at the front, her lace peignoir assumed over her delicate shoulders, and perhaps the merest touch of colour applied to the cheeks. She looked, as usual, the most desirable woman in the world, and Mr Wilbert Fenton, so long a rake, could never stop giving thanks for his luck in marrying her.

'Oh, Wilbert, Miss Fleet has written to say she has quit the London house to travel to Durant at last!'

'Felicity home ! No doubt,' he drawled, 'you have arranged for us to go to Durant at the earliest possibility.'

'Well, of course! And you need not pretend that you are not just as eager to see our dear girl as I am.'

'I hope Miss Fleet is not embarrassed by the newlyweds.' Fenton said, nibbling on a slice of apple. 'If like us, they are apt not to want interruption.'

'She lived very happily with them in London. Felicity told me she was discretion itself.'

'I'm sure she was, poor little soul. And she'll be happier with Felicity than with the dreadful Lady Ellingham.' Mr Fenton now nibbled his wife's fingers, which that lady regarded with indulgence.

'She could hardly,' Lady Aurora said, reminiscently, 'be less.'

Chapter Two

A Bear Bursts In

A loud and booming voice shouted 'Pollock!' and an unnaturally tall and imposing figure entered the inn taproom, dipping his head to enter, then blocking the light from the entire doorframe.

'Oh!' cried a timid little lady, dropping her chocolate over the bodice of her best, if rather dull, grey poplin gown. The giant stopped and regarded both her and the large stain that was spreading over the front of her dress. She was a very small, slight lady of perhaps forty years, with a thin face that was given light by the enormous brown eyes that filled most of it. For the rest, her lips were a trifle thin, her nose of no particular interest, her hair an undistinguished brown pulled back into a simple knot and adorned by the plainest of muslin caps, with only some pin-tucks to give it shape.

'Where's Pollock?' he demanded, his eyes firing at her from beneath beetle brows. He was around fifty years, if she was any judge, and it was a striking rather than handsome face. A shock of wiry hair around his dark features. Deep set dark eyes dominated his strong square face, making him look like the villain from one of her favourite Gothic novels. His large frame and barrel chest was further exaggerated by the many-caped driving coat he wore. His cravat was carelessly knotted, his boots dusty. He was like a once fashionable man gone to seed.

Urged to speak, the lady seemed embarrassed not to be able to help him. 'Is — is that the name of the proprietor? I'm afraid, sir, that I do not know.' Distractedly, she dabbed at her dress with her napkin, with little effect.

The massive man looked down at her pursuit. 'What happened to your dress?'

'It ... it is nothing, sir.'

'Did I make you jump? My niece is forever saying I should lower my voice.' He looked down at the stain once more. 'You should change your dress.' This was issued in the same commanding tone, which made her jump again.

'I cannot. But mayhap I can dab away...'

'No other dress?'

She wished he would not shout so. 'No,' she excused herself. 'You see, I am travelling to my friend's house with only my night things, for my trunk has been sent ahead.'

'You cannot travel in that—' he indicated her dress, to her intense mortification, saying so at a volume that she was surprised did not raise the house. But the tap boy seemed to have disappeared, and the inn, at this early hour, was remarkably deserted. They were quite alone. 'Come with me!'

'I ... I—'

He had turned and reached the double doors to the taproom, which were left open, then turned back to her. 'Come!' he ordered.

The lady automatically jumped to her feet, and followed meekly, picking up her cloak and bonnet as she did so. Very few steps took her to his side and he looked down at her appraisingly. 'As I thought, your shoulders at my waist...' She thought she saw a tear in his eye, but he began to walk again, and she ran after him, taking two steps for the giant's every one. She put on her bonnet as they left the inn, and flew her cloak over her shoulders as they walked. A high-perch phaeton stood in the yard and when he had reached it, the giant turned and made a bow. 'The name is Balfour. May I know yours?'

'I am Miss Fleet.' And so saying, the little lady made a curtsy.

'Now that we are introduced,' he said, grasping her by the waist, and lifting her into the phaeton. She gasped and shook even more, holding onto the side of the carriage. 'Never been in a high-perch number, eh?' he said, in a booming voice she supposed was meant to be heartening. 'Hold on and it won't kill you.' He jumped in beside her (his weight causing her to bounce on the seat) and released the reins.

Miss Fleet, adjusting her grey bonnet with dignity, said quietly but firmly, 'I have been a passenger in the Viscount Durant's high-perch phaeton on many occasions.' Her bravery overtook her, and she trembled once more.

'Ho! So you know Sebastian?' said the man called Balfour, manoeuvring the horses through the tall inn-yard gates.

'I am travelling to his home.'

The man was kept occupied by a cart coming out precipitately from a farm road. Once they had gotten around it and no wheels had ended in a ditch, Miss Fleet made a shy enquiry.

'Excuse me sir, but where are you taking me, and for what reason?'

The man gave a shout of laughter. 'You should ask that before you get into a carriage with a fellow, not after.'

'I did not precisely *get into* the carriage—' she protested. Then she seemed to tremble again. 'I beg your pardon.'

He took a second to look down at her, and the big harsh face seemed to be laughing. 'For what, pray?'

'I ... I—' she could not think of precisely why. 'For my impertinence,' she ventured.

He laughed uproariously. 'Oh, mighty impertinent you are.' He wiped a hand over streaming eyes. 'You should strive to rein in your impertinence at all costs.' He slapped his knee at his own good joke, and then he made a turn with the phaeton and began to make his way to a tidy manor house a half-mile in the distance.

Miss Fleet clutched at her reticule, glancing sideways at the edifice. The man, not the manor house.

A groom ran forward to grasp the reins as they reached the house, and the tall front door was already open, a liveried servant in attendance. Her companion jumped down and while Miss Fleet was deciding how she might make an attempt with dignity, he was at her side reaching for her waist again, and she had the heady feeling of being swung down without her volition once more. He looked down at her.

'A little pocket Venus!' he whispered.

Miss Fleet looked up at him with her very large eyes, hardly believing her ears, but trembling never the less.

'Oh, not you!' he muttered and let her go, walking up the steps to his manor, and greeting the dogs who ran to his side.

Miss Fleet followed, at a pace, but with a wary eye on the dogs.

As she caught up with him, she heard him say to the footman. 'Send for Evans! And bring some refreshments to the blue room.'

'The *blue* room sir?'

'*Yes!*' he fairly shouted. 'The blue room.'

'Your Lordship!' The footman bowed in an apologetic fashion.

The room whose door he opened was indeed blue, with pale blue silk on the walls, and on the upholstery of the delicately wrought furniture set about the room. In her enchantment, Miss Fleet stopped on the threshold, quite forgetting to be terrified. It was a lady's sitting room, she thought, but quite the prettiest she had ever seen. It was of a modest size, a little larger than merely cosy, with one big window of perhaps sixty panes taking up the middle of a wall, and the most heavenly curtains at the windows: on a blue ground, humming birds of every possible hue flew around. The furniture was trimmed in gilt, two elegant chairs, one considerably larger than the other, sat on each side of a charming fireplace, an escritoire was on one wall near the window, with everything a lady might want to write with, and to add to the perfection, a white-painted and gilded harpsichord was on the other side of the room. The ceiling was high, of course, and some cherubs held up each corner, and clustered around the ceiling rose.

'How lovely!' she sighed, despite herself.

She noted then that he had stopped, seemingly stranded in the middle of the Chinese carpet, and he looked around saying, 'Well. Well! Yes, well, well!' as though he did not know quite what to say. He too seemed to be looking around the room, and he put his hand to his chest as though in pain.

Miss Fleet ran forward, touching his arm and guiding him to the larger of the two chairs by the empty fireplace. 'Sit, sir!' she said, 'Please, you are not well.'

'Nonsense!' he barked. 'I am very well.' But he sat nevertheless, dropping precariously onto the chair, which no longer looked large.

'May I ring for some water? Is there perhaps some medicine ...?'

'You are eye to eye with me now ...' he seemed to look at her from a great distance, 'and your voice is as soft as mine is loud ...'

It was like the moment when he had said those strange words to her outside. He was not really speaking to her.

'You sent for me, sir?' said a stentorian voice, and Miss Fleet turned quickly, jumping at the tone. It reminded her, in tone if not in accent, of the terrible Lady Ellingham, to whom she had been a companion until very lately. So swiftly did she turn that she almost fell over, but a large steadying hand righted her. She had been touched by male hand more in the last hour than in any time since the death of her papa.

The maid, because thus she undoubtedly was, stood very tall in the doorway with her hands crossed before her.

'Take this lady, Miss ... eh... Fleet, to Her Ladyship's room and give her the blue muslin.'

'Her Ladyship's gowns are packed, my lord,' said the tall maid with a sour look.

His Lordship stood up. 'Then *unpack* them, Evans, and help the lady change. Then see to her dress.'

'Very well, sir,' said the maid and turned saying, 'this way, miss!'

Miss Fleet followed her, since she could not for the moment think what else to do. His Lordship's burst of anger seemed to have brought him back to himself, so she had no qualms in leaving him. She wished to protest that it was not at all necessary, but she did not wish to disagree with him in front of his servant.

The maid led the way up a broad staircase, emanating displeasure. Miss Fleet was almost overpowered by it, but tried to straighten her back. If her dear Felicity could face such outright aggression as she had in the last year before her engagement to Viscount Durant, when the dreadful, untrue rumours had been spread, then so would she. She was no longer Lady Ellingham's unpaid companion, she was a friend and (albeit distant) relation to a viscountess and possessed an exorbitant sum of money in her reticule given to her by the viscount before he left upon his wedding trip. It was given to allow her to make any purchases she might want and to order a chaise-and-four, as she was to join them (after the two months of the trip) on their country estate. But a chaise-and-four was hardly necessary, she had felt. She was used to the stage, and she could not think of anything she needed to buy beyond some toiletries for the journey. She had been left in their London house in the interim, with servants to see to her every comfort – most especially enjoined so to do by the new viscountess. This gentle treatment had, she supposed, beefed up her spirits a little, for she resolved not to be beaten by a sour face. She had seen a great many sour faces in her previous existence, and no doubt she could cope.

She thought, too, about the dresses being packed up. Was Lady Balfour to go on a trip? But no, Miss Fleet believed, by some little things that she had observed, that perhaps Lady Balfour had recently died.

Evans opened the door to a bedchamber quite as charming as the sitting room. She went directly to a carved wooden box, searched through the tissue paper layers, and found a blue muslin gown, which she shook out.

'I cannot wear that!' said Miss Fleet. 'It is too lovely...' She had considered the looking for a dress rather doomed as she had climbed the stairs. Unless there was a full paper of pins to be used, her height made it quite impossible for the lending of dresses that her dear Felicity had suggested. ('Never mind, Euphemia,' as the viscountess now called her, 'we'll have some made up when we reach home.') But as she looked at the dress before her, a figured muslin in the same blue as the sitting room, over a satin slip, Miss Fleet felt it beyond her position entirely. The detailed embroidery on the bodice, the sleeves and around the hem made it a very expensive, but still simple gown.

'She did look lovely in it.'

There was a wistfulness in the maid's tone that made Miss Fleet ask, 'Her Ladyship is dead?'

'The baroness died these two years since.'

She did not speak again, but her demeanour as she untied Miss Fleet's laced back and removed her stained but sturdy poplin, causing the heavenly blue to fall over her head, let Miss Fleet know how undeserving of the dress she was. But she was astonished to see herself in the mirror when she wore it. She looked … different. Not a poor relation anymore. She had not let her dear Felicity buy her clothes, though Mrs Aurora Fenton, acting as Felicity's guardian, had insisted on having her outfitted for the wedding, at least. That dress, though lovely, Miss Fleet had insisted be quite plain, like herself. *This* dress was made for a Lady of the Manor.

And what is more, beyond the need for a pin or two at the side of her bodice, (for she knew herself to be preternaturally thin) it fitted her precisely. Her serviceable but now very plain-looking boots poked beneath the hemline just the right amount.

The maid looked down too. 'The boots are stained, too, miss. You'd best give them to me. She moved to another coffer where she lifted some cream satin slippers. 'These might do, miss.' While these would complete the outfit, the tone was still hostile. Miss Fleet wondered ghoulishly if there were poisoned needles inside and the maid was in a plot to kidnap her. But she was no young girl to be kidnapped for either money or beauty. She took them therefore, just because the pearls sewn above the toes needed to be caressed. 'They will not do for travelling,' she said, with as straight a back as she could muster, 'so I must not wear them. How beautiful they are.'

'Her Ladyship herself stitched the tops, and I simply put them together.'

'But the stitching is very fine, Evans. Very fine.'

'I'll get your boots and dress in an hour, miss,' said Evans, in a rather gentler voice. 'Just you put these on.'

But Miss Fleet's feet were rather smaller than the mistress's, and Evans had to stuff the toes with cotton, which made it just possible to keep them on. 'I could attach a ribbon, miss, er,'

'Fleet. I am Miss Fleet.'

'Miss Fleet. If you thought you was — were — going to fall in them.'

'No. I don't suppose I shall. It seems a shame to spoil them with a ribbon.'

Evans stood, brushing at her apron. 'As to that, Miss Fleet. It is nice to see them worn again.' Her voice caught. 'From the back, you could almost be—'

'Thank you Evans. I'm sorry I — thank you.' And Miss Fleet made her way to the blue salon once more, walking carefully in the too-large slippers.

She hesitated before she entered. She had left the maid with tears in her eyes — what might she do to the husband? But a mirror next to the door saved her, for reflected in it was a portrait that hung behind her, glimpsed through the doors of a grander salon. Miss Fleet turned, and glided towards the portrait. It was of a young woman wearing the fashions of thirty years ago. In a sylvan setting, wearing a frothy muslin gown, much fuller than those of today, the young beauty sat in an enormous brimmed straw hat with broad yellow ribbons caught under her chin in a charming bow. She had startling, naughty blue eyes, and her blond curls were wide beneath her bonnet, then coaxed into a ringlet over one shoulder. Her gaze was both challenging and merry, her stature diminutive, and one tiny, lazy hand played with a pup's ear as others gambolled around her. A pocket Venus indeed. Euphemia Fleet felt a tug of sorrow for the man who now awaited her in the blue salon, at losing not just such a beauty, but such a force of life. She stopped worrying that she would conjure up his beloved too well. Yes, the inhabited dress might cause him pause, but *she* was no beauty. She turned away, back towards the blue room. As she raised her hand to tap at the door before she entered, she glanced in the mirror once more. It was as if Her Ladyship was urging her on.

He had been sitting in the grand blue chair as she left him, and so she found him once more: one hand at his chest, looking deep into the flames of a fire that now burned cheerily in the grate. His breaths rasped and were shallow, but he looked up as she entered, and he stood, his eyes alight, clutching at his chest again. 'My lady!' his other enormous arm reached for her, and he collapsed into the chair.

'You *are* unwell,' said Miss Fleet, gliding towards him hurriedly. There was a sweat on his brow as she touched it, and she hardly knew she had taken the liberty. She loosened his cravat, then rang a bell, which was almost instantly answered by a hall footman in green livery. It seemed as though the baron could not breathe. She was bent over the giant and his lips were forming something that she had to lower herself to hear.

'Her gown. You look so like in figure, so like...'

'Yes, but it is only her gown, not she. Hush now—' she turned to the servant, 'Your master is ill—' she began.

'Begging your pardon miss, but I'll just fetch his draught.'

'Yes. Do that first.'

The giant was saying more. His voice came in hoarse tones, just audible as she was so near. 'Lady Balfour was so beautiful in that gown, so lovely in everything she did. You move like her.'

'I'm honoured. But I don't think it does you good to think of it just now. Close your eyes, and breathe deeply.' His breath had become shallower and laboured, and she looked around the room for some water that she might apply to his brow.

A neat man hurried in, carrying what Miss Fleet sincerely hoped was His Lordship's draught. He poured it, hardly looking at her, and forced the milky liquid down his throat.

'Dammit Tinder!' Miss Fleet was glad to hear that his complaint was nearly at his normal volume.

'Sir! I thought you unconscious!'

'No, merely obeying Miss Fleet's adjuration to close my eyes. She is afraid I'll be undone by the sight of her in the blue gown.' He grinned toward Miss Fleet, who was hovering on the other side. 'Do tell her that these attacks are unforeseeable,' he said to Tinder. 'Though the sight of her is enough to raise the senses.' He smiled at her then, in a different way, a way that no man had ever — was he *flirting* with her? It seemed flirting of an advanced kind, for though his face was only now regaining its colour, the lazy smile was one that she had seen on Viscount Durant's face as he indicated he wished to be alone with Felicity, his viscountess. It had made her blush to see, though naturally she had affected not to notice, and to have business elsewhere in the house. But now the colour washed over her face in the hottest blush she had ever known.

But this too was addressed to a memory, she reminded herself, not to her.

'You should rest, sir,' said the small valet in his knee breeches and neat cutaway coat, throwing Miss Fleet a rather jealous glance. 'Are you well enough to let us take you to your room?'

'No, Tinder. Leave me.'

'Bring some water, some flannel, and a little brandy, if you please,' ordered Miss Fleet gently.

He had closed his eyes again, and now looked up at her. 'If that's for me, I'll allow you to tend me only if you will sit in the other chair afterwards.'

'I cannot!' she protested, 'I really *must* go. My coach leaves the inn at noon.' But the valet pulled on her sleeve.

'It's best to agree with him and keep him calm, miss, after an attack,' he whispered. 'If he gets upset, then it can flare up again.' Aloud, he said. 'I will bring back your brandy, my lord. But just a glass to sip, mind.'

'And I interrupted the lady's refreshments at the inn, bring something, Tinder.'

'I—' she began.

'Do not say me nay.' He closed his eyes and smiled again. 'I said that to my lady once.'

The brandy and flannel were brought, and Tinder set a footstool for his master, taking off his massive boots with remarkable efficiency. It was apparent that the giant did not favour the skin-tight mode of today's fashion. Miss Fleet was not used to the sight of male stockinged-feet, and was rather glad when the valet draped the thin quilted cover over him. He cooled his master's brow, and left the room reluctantly at his master's gesture.

'You're sitting in her chair,' he said, amazedly. 'You look like you belong there.'

'I most assuredly belong elsewhere: namely on the stage-coach going to Durant.'

He smiled at her. 'Your first sign of temper. Mild, but I liked it.' His voice was going stronger, but he rested back in the chair. A tray arrived, and he watched intermittently as she ate from it delicately. 'So lovely,' he said, and fell asleep. Miss Fleet's cheeks were tinged with colour and she felt inordinately moved that a man should speak so to her — but she knew he was addressing another.

She sat with him for another hour, listening as his breath slowed and deepened, and felt his head to check that he had no fever. He looked so like a wounded bear and she was free to take stock of him. His hands were bigger than her body from chin to waist. She held one briefly, and her own hand disappeared entirely. The hands were shapely though, perhaps he too could play the harpsichord like his lady? His great barrel chest seemed like the strongest in all the world, and yet his insides were capable of laying him so low.

She felt pity for him. He had obviously indulged his lady's taste in many things. The pretty chair she sat in was more suited to her size than any she had ever known. It had a foreshortened seat, so that she could rest back, and lowered legs so that her feet did not dangle in the air. She could imagine the other little lady here, in her fine dresses, sitting opposite her big Bear, discussing their days. He obviously missed her so much that seeing another wear a dress of hers made him ill. When she was satisfied that he was somewhat better, she left the room.

'Could you send Evans to me?' said Miss Fleet to the butler, as she walked from the hall. He was a slight but tall man, and his eyes met hers with more warmth than his position might usually allow. All the household must be concerned about their master. Miss Fleet smiled at him comfortingly, conveying she hoped that all would be well with Lord Balfour. 'I'll be in the other salon. His Lordship is asleep.' She crossed the hall and entered into the salon of the portrait, elegantly furnished in pale shades of green. She was never going to catch the stagecoach now, she feared, and was doomed to spend another night at the inn. The Durants were not expecting her on a particular day, thankfully, but she felt herself to be in limbo, her simple plan averted.

She sat for some time, awaiting Evans, her eyes with little to do but take in all the taste and thought of comfort that had gone into the planning of this room. She judged that this part of the house was more modern, in the style of Mr Adam, than the ancient building attached at the side. The barony was medieval, she supposed. But the room had a light modern elegance, with a degree of comfortable touches, some pillows, some footstools and tables placed carefully. Some screens were dotted around, too, to be easily moved to exclude any draughts. A book placed on the little table by the fire suggested that reading was not limited to the library. This house was a home, and not simply a denizen of good taste. She picked up the book idly, and noted that it was in Greek, sadly beyond her education. Only gentlemen learned Greek and Latin, said Papa, and moreover forbade her reading even in English, beyond the bible and religious works. She descried some story in both, and so was ripe for the novel, as soon as she had left home. Her father would have been shocked, and she read each new book with a frisson of guilt and enjoyment.

Finally, she began to feel that the maid was delaying to some purpose, and she opened the door of the chamber to summon another servant to see what was amiss, when she saw Evans in the hallway with Tinder, who might actually be whispering to her. She cried 'Evans!' and the woman arrived with a return to her more closed-off demeanour.

'Please bring me my dress and boots, I need to depart quite soon.'

'The blue muslin dress my master desires that you keep, miss. Your own is not quite dry. Nor are the boots.'

Euphemia Fleet flushed. Surely the boots, at least, would have dried out by the kitchen range.

'The master is calling for you.'

Chapter Three

Tending the Sick

It was to an upper room, close to the one she had already entered, that Miss Fleet was ushered. She was accompanied by Evans and Tinder as she crossed the threshold, so she felt adequately chaperoned, though nervous at entering a gentleman's bedchamber. His Lordship was propped up on a vast bed, his hair a mane around him as he rested against the pillows. He was dressed in a white night shirt with an open collar, which displayed a sliver of hirsute chest beneath his powerful neck column. Miss Fleet averted her eyes quickly, shaken by the masculine musk of the room and by the physicality of the massive figure on the bed. She stopped so abruptly that Evans had difficulty to avoid falling into her.

Then Miss Fleet looked at the grey face of the man who held his hand out to her. She moved soundlessly forward, as was her wont, and she touched his hand for a fraction of a second. It had almost been, for a moment, like the hand of her papa on his death bed, seeking solace.

His breathing was laboured, but he managed to say, 'Pray do not be angry with me, dear lady.'

'Hush now, my lord. I am not angry. I have only missed my coach, but I shall return to the inn presently, if your groom will drive me, and you may rest easy.' She looked at his great dark eyes shyly, but compassionately. She was a little concerned about his colour. She found herself moving a wisp of wiry hair from his eyes, in a gesture that looked like a caress. 'I beg your pardon,' she said, her voice a squeak once more, and pulled her arms to her body.

'It is not for that I apologise,' the giant was saying. She looked at Tinder, who met her eye from the other side of the bed, where he had tried to apply a compress to Lord Balfour's head and had been shrugged off. Tinder's eyes held a grave warning. 'It is that I had your valise sent over here from the inn.' He saw her shock and repossessed himself of her hand. 'I am a selfish beast, my lady said many a time. But your presence calms me, Miss Fleet. And the sawbones tell me that I need—' he paused to take several painful breaths, 'to be calm when my attacks occur. Will you not stay?'

'Your Lordship—' began Miss Fleet.

'Miss,' said Tinder, in a voice of warning, 'Evans has had a truckle bed made up in your room. She will stay with you this night. And my lord has asked me to advise Lord Durant that you make a visit here.'

'Are you — *very* angry?' he asked, his eyes looking so like a lost puppy's that Miss Fleet was moved. She suspected that she was being manipulated in some way, but she was not sufficiently habituated to being considered *at all,* to avoid being flattered by His Lordship's concern for her feelings.

'I am not. But I think you would be better served to rest sir, and let me return to the inn. It may be that seeing another in the garments of the late Lady Balfour has brought on the attack...'

'Perhaps,' he said, and trapped the hand she sought to remove with his giant paw. 'But I am calmer now. Your voice calms me. If Evans sets a chair for you, will you not sit and talk to me?'

Evans did so, and Miss Fleet, being given back her hand, acquiesced and sat. It was late afternoon now, and the sun was setting, so Tinder had lit a candle and placed it on his master's nightstand, between Miss Fleet and him. The servants moved to chairs set against the walls in opposite dark corners, Tinder to continue to attend his master and Evans stayed too, as a chaperone of sorts, she supposed. Miss Fleet could almost feel that she and His Lordship were all alone in the candle's glow. 'But what on earth can I say?' she mused aloud.

'It does not matter. Tell me about your life, Miss Fleet. Who are your family?'

'Of close family, I have only a sister and her husband left in all the world, I'm afraid. She married when Papa was still alive, and moved from the rectory to London to marry a lawyer, Mr Fishbourne, whose clients, I believe, are mainly wool-traders. They have a very modest home, and after Papa died, I went to live with them, but it did not suit. I took up rather too much space you see, and—'

His Lordship's cry of '*You?*' gave way to a laugh and then a cough, and Miss Fleet found herself patting his hand in comfort as she had her father's in his last days. She smiled at his joke though, and said, 'Well I am small, but they still had to devote their only spare chamber to me and when his mother came to visit, it was indeed awkward.

'Did your father leave you unprovided for?'

'Well, he had very little, you see, and of course my cousin in India inherited.'

'I do not understand. Was it entailed property?'

'Not at all. But gentlemen must inherit, is it not so? My papa advised me, on his last days, that I must stay with my sister, or seek employment as a governess.'

Something had made the gentleman's breath shorten once more, and Tinder darted forward, but he gestured him away. 'And — then?' he managed with difficulty.

'This is all very dull sir. I was seeking a post as a governess, when my brother-in-law remembered that Papa had mentioned that a second cousin of ours had married a Lord Ellingham, and he wrote to Lady Ellingham about my —' Miss Fleet looked into her lap and began pleating the folds of blue satin, '— straightened circumstances, and she was happy I stay with her, so all was well,' she added brightly.

'In a post of companion?'

'Well, I wasn't employed as such, but I suppose I performed the duties. I ever tried to be grateful to Lady Ellingham for the roof and the nourishment that she provided me.' Her voice had become small again and there was a short silence.

'How long for?'

'Ten years.'

His voice lowered. 'Was it *very* dreadful?'

The kindness in his voice almost overwhelmed her and she said, 'She was a little eccentric, of course. But the happiest thing occurred. Last year, another relative of Lady Ellingham's came to stay for a few weeks, and she taught me to laugh a little.'

'What about your situation was amusing?' he asked.

'Well, Felicity found so much amusing.' Her eyes began to look a little timidly mischievous, and the dark eyes from the bed held hers. 'Do you know, Lady Ellingham wore the same bonnet that she'd had bought for her on her honeymoon, for *forty years*?'

'I've heard of her, of course. Quite mad, they say! And you spent *ten years* there?' There were breaths between each sentence, and he seemed a little angry.

She said, reassuringly, 'But I saw my sister once a week for an hour and I was also permitted to attend the circulation library. I had every new novel, I assure you. It was my sheer delight, for Lady Ellingham *meant* to read them but didn't, so I was quite free to read once she was abed, or out for the evening.'

He seemed to detect her real enthusiasm, and he asked her, 'Tell me the story of the last novel you read, for it is such a while since I read one. I am tired now, so you may be for me like my old nurse as a child, who when I was ill, would tell me stories at night until I went to sleep.'

'You may not share my taste sir. I shall not tell you the last, but my favourite tale. It is about a young man named Vivaldi and his love for Ellena. But a wicked priest wishes to part them ...' It was an hour later when the first scene of the story reached its blood-curdling climax, and Miss Fleet heard the soft snoring of sleep, with a calmer breath, and she got up as silently as she had entered, and moved from the room.

Evans showed her to a room much further along the corridor, thankfully not Lady Balfour's chamber, and helped her undress. Miss Fleet, living in the viscount's house for the last weeks, was now accustomed to this attention, and let her. 'I have to tell you, miss, that when I attempted to remove the stain from the bodice of your gown it became bleached. I am most sorry.'

She was brushing Miss Fleet's hair before the dressing mirror and Miss Fleet met her eyes kindly. 'There is no need to worry, Evans. Lay it out for tomorrow. I shall put my cloak over it as I travel on tomorrow's stage.' It occurred to her that Evans, too, had heard the tale of her position in life: hardly higher than a servant's. There should have been a diminution of respect in her bearing, but incredibly, it seemed to have increased. 'Is there an earlier one on the morrow?'

'I do not — think so, miss,' said Evans, averting her eyes, 'But I imagined that you would wish to see how His Lordship fares in the morning before you go leaving in the afternoon, so I have cut out the bleached part of the bodice and I am going to insert some nice fabric I have to replace it. It won't be quite ready first thing, miss,' she hesitated. 'Unless you were wishful I stay up this night?'

'Of course not, Evans. You are quite correct that I will wish to stay in the morning, though I do think His Lordship's breathing was better, do not you?'

'Yes miss,' agreed Evans, and went to pull back the bed clothes.

Miss Fleet sighed when she thought she might even now be going to sleep at Durant Court, but she did know that the Bear's intentions had been good, and that she was glad somehow to be of use to him.

Chapter Four
A Tour of the Gardens

Early as Miss Fleet arose, Evans rose earlier, and delivered some hot chocolate in a tiny cup with roses on it, to her in bed.

'I know you wish to say *"careful"* to me Evans,' Miss Fleet said, in her quiet way, 'but I assure you that if Lord Balfour's voice does not scare me to death, I shall not spill it.'

Evans gave her twisted grin. 'No guarantee of that in this house, miss,' she said wryly.

Miss Fleet got up and washed, and saw that the maid had laid another dress out for her to wear. She looked at it admiringly, but dubiously. Would yet another inhabited dress be any good for His Lordship's condition? It was evident that these artefacts had a profound effect on him. But Evans was now calmly sewing a new bodice onto Miss Fleet's grey poplin, and the blue dress was nowhere to be seen. It did not seem worth complaining of, so she put on the new gown. It was a more practical morning dress, Miss Fleet considered, with long gauze sleeves and gauze above the low bodice, made up to the throat. But the simple white muslin, sprigged with yellow primroses, seemed much too young for her. As Evans buttoned it at the back, Euphemia Fleet observed herself. Evans had done something with her hair. She had let a lock or two escape, and had seemed to twirl it idly about her fingers, even as she told Miss Fleet about the breakfast awaiting her, and the weather today. The hair now made little ringlets at each side of her face. It had seemed that Evans had formed the same simple coil as she usually achieved herself, but it was more expertly done and gave her a crown of hair that gave her another, welcome, inch in height. It was lovely, but Miss Fleet resolutely put her cap on top.

She came down the steps and heard the booming tones of the Bear. 'Well, Miss Fleet. I am all agog to know how Florian rescued Ellena.'

She entered a smaller salon, where everything had been set for a breakfast as cosy as any in Viscount Durant's London house, but of a volume befitting a Bear. She regarded the great figure carefully, even as she said, 'Good morning, Baron. I trust you are well?' He was close-shaved and his shirt was starched and smart. His great frame was also housed in a light coloured waistcoat to the neck and a blue superfine coat over very clean buckskins and boots. He bowed from the waist, and she saw that the dress had had an effect, but his skin was no longer grey and his lungs seemed to be the great bellows that she had first heard them as. She was relieved.

'Very well, but I shall have a relapse if you do not continue,' he boomed at her playfully.

She laughed shyly, and began, over coffee, rolls, fruit and some slivers of beef, to tell him of the awful machinations of the heinous cleric, Schedoni. As with her friend Felicity, she was apt to get carried away in the telling, and so it proved. The most ghastly parts of the tale she told in relished detail, gesturing with her hands to her throat in a dramatic way, making the fainting motion of Ellena, and the terrifying eyes of Schedoni. The baron laughed, and he laughed heartily.

At one point she saw the butler, Tinder, and Evans all in the hall looking at them through the open door with interest. She recollected herself, and returned to her quiet, unobtrusive self.

'Would you care to see the garden, Miss Fleet?' When he saw her hesitate, he added, 'There is no hurry. My coachman will take you to Sebastian's house, it is but three hours from here.'

'I could not—' she began.

'And *I* could not let you go on the stage after the kindness you have shown me. And Sebastian would not forgive me.' She was still hesitant. 'I cannot imagine he expected that you would use the stagecoach as your mode of transport when he asked you to join them, now did he?'

She sighed. 'No he did not. Thank you sir, I will accept your kind offer.'

He held out his great arm in a courtly manner, 'The gardens then?'

She rose and took his arm, and though she was piqued by the thought that he was really offering his arm to another, she still enjoyed the unwarranted attention. She knew he only did so that he might walk beside a slight figure that reminded him of a beloved wife, and therefore she would repress her feelings of hurt. What price a sting to her spirit if she could offer that little time on memory's pathways to a grieving man? It was only a morning walk, after all.

The gardens were past their best, she could see, but there was more than enough in the carefully tended walkways for Miss Fleet to really enjoy. Tall hedges screened sheltered walks and opened into secret little havens where benches had been placed to allow yet another sylvan scene to be viewed. One of these little clearings, which was almost totally enclosed, allowed the warm sun in and kept the wind out, and Miss Fleet nodded happily as the baron raised an eyebrow to a bench placed there. 'It is so peaceful. Almost like my father's empty church, where I sat as a girl.'

'I think it my favourite place,' the big man sighed.

Miss Fleet said quietly, 'Do you want to speak of her, sir?'

'Not really. She was everything to me and I lost her.' The voice was low and deep, and Miss Fleet's arm, still somehow entwined with his, dared to squeeze a little, before pulling away a little guiltily.

'I am so sorry for your loss. But you only have to look at God's new day to know there is a great deal left here for you.'

'I assure you, I am not often morbid. I had not been in the blue room for two years you know, but I had such a fancy to see you there that I braved it. It was a little too much all at once, and at these times my blasted lungs seize up.'

'It must be very frightening.'

'No. Just dashed annoying. And it sets Tinder off into cursed nursemaid's behaviour and I will not have it!' His brows were drawn down, but the memory of his attack was between them and as their eyes met somehow they smiled.

'Tinder is very devoted.'

'Yes, damn him. I'm minded to get myself a valet who does the job and doesn't give a—' he stopped the oath, but she had jumped in.

'Indeed. But you will not.'

'Of course not. I'm stuck with him.' He sighed 'Enough about my schoolboy complaint. How long do you spend at Sebastian's?'

'Indefinitely. I am to make my home there with my friend, the viscountess.' She stood up, and they began to walk on, and she looked at him carefully. 'I suppose you think me selfish, to invade the home of such newlyweds? But they were so insistent.'

'No, indeed,' he said, looking ahead, but taking her hand to rest on his arm again. 'You have earned your pardon after ten years with

Lady Ellingham.' He pulled her around gently back towards the house saying, 'Look! This is the best prospect of the house, I believe. What do you think of it, my dear lady?'

It was a fine prospect indeed, in three-quarter view of the front and one side, with the light stone glinting almost white in the sun today. A nearby stream was visible, as well as some of the prettiest of the garden walks. It was not intimidating, but charming. She wondered if the gardens, which mixed the formal and the informal: creeping roses on a side wall and wisteria clamouring over fences, (glorious in summer, she supposed) offsetting the geometric flower beds at the front, was the product of the late Lady Balfour's taste. It was rather like the house with its Palladian geometry mixing with the informality of extra pillows and footstools in the salon. 'It is quite perfect.'

He gave a bear growl that seemed, in feeling, to be more of a purr, and said with pride, 'So do I. Many houses are grander, but I would not swap a one for Balfour Court.'

They moved ahead a minute, and Balfour asked her to relate her knowledge of Viscount Durant and the young wife whom he had not yet met. Skirting the unfounded rumours around Felicity's reputation, she described her meeting with the young girl in Lady Ellingham's house and their shared love of novels, and how Felicity had been saved from the old mad woman's quirks by moving into Lady Aurora's house with her and Mr Wilbert Fenton. 'She became the rage of town, I believe, for she is so beautiful. But still we met each week in the circulating library, and she told me all her news. It was as though I went to all the balls and splendid occasions myself.' Her eyes shone up at him, and he patted her arm companionably. Even these slight attentions made her blush and tremor, but she continued talking of her dear Felicity to calm herself. 'And she had a way of making me less afraid of Lady Ellingham, too, for she had such merry eyes when

Her Ladyship said something stern. Meeting my dear Felicity changed my life, even before the viscount and she insisted that I leave Lady Ellingham's. I did so, expressing to Her Ladyship how very grateful I was for her bounty in the intervening years, but she was very angry with me, and though I have gone to her house since, she will not admit me.'

'If that grey poplin dress is an example of her bounty, I do not think a deal of it.'

'Oh well, I did not go out in town, you know, so she felt I had no need of new clothes, and she was quite right. And dear Felicity has asked more than once to refurbish my wardrobe, but I will not allow it. It is too much.'

He stopped then and undid the strings of her cloak, standing very close to her as he did so. She held her breath. He was too close, too large not to feel intimidated. She could not resume breathing until he finished, and he swung her cloak over his arm. 'Now, that dress becomes you so much better,' he said. She looked down at the gaily coloured flowers to hide her blushes. 'Lady Balfour,' she agreed firmly, as though to depress her own and his flights of fancy, 'had very good taste. It is very lovely, but it is too young for me. A spring gown for a spring maiden.'

'It is lovely, and you look lovely in it.' He looked down at her and she trembled at the kind pity in his eyes, 'As though your own spring had come once more.'

'Please do not say such things, Lord Balfour. You mean to be kind, but I assure you, you are not. I am plain and nearly forty, and I know it well.'

He hesitated. 'I will not talk on this subject and spoil our walk, though I could take issue with you. Tell me more about your beloved

Felicity. I will be happy to know that my friend has such a prize, even if she is only half so beautiful and good as you say.'

'Oh, I am not given to exaggeration,' said Miss Fleet.

'You? Who sent shivers down my back at your retelling of Mrs Radcliffe's novel?'

'But I assure you, it is *just* that terrifying!' said Miss Fleet, seriously. But she saw that he laughed at her and they moved on, and she continued to talk of her friend, the new viscountess. 'Before she left for Europe she said to me "Euphemia" (for that is my given name) "you have always said nothing ever happens to you. Well after your move to Durant, see what adventures we will have together." She smiled up at him, her head almost bent to her back. 'Look what an adventure I shall have to tell her about before I even arrive there.'

'And what title should you give the tale?'

'Euphemia and the Wounded Bear!' she said at once.

'Euphemia meets a bear with a thorn in his paw and pulls it right out. And then he becomes a handsome prince, I heard such a folk tale once. You are to be disappointed in the transformation to a prince, I suppose, but you do weave a magical spell.'

'Do not be absurd!' she smiled a little, for since Felicity had left, she had missed being teased.

'Euphemia,' he mused. 'I have never known a Euphemia. I like the name very well. It means well-spoken, in the Greek, I think. And you speak only fair words.'

They had reached a little fence, designed to keep a few sheep in a paddock to make pets of them, she thought. There was stile before it, which she found herself lifted onto in a minute, by dint of his hands once more around her waist. 'Sir!' she protested. 'You must not.'

He had vaulted the fence nimbly and was reaching over to take her waist once more, but she pushed his arms wide. 'This may be what you wished to do with your wife, but it is not at all appropriate to do so with—'

'Oh no,' Lord Balfour said as he bore down on her, 'with my wife I wished to do like *so!*' In a fraction of a second he had tipped her slight form over his shoulder and he was running like a youth across the field, with her screaming some reprimand that was indecipherable. His big bear arm grasped the back of her knees, her bonnet became dislodged from her head and she saw her blue cape fly over a hedge. It was insane, absurd, scandalous behaviour, but the headiest feeling of her whole life. Her hair was falling from its pins, she must look ridiculous, and suddenly a crack appeared in her personality. She laughed and laughed. As soon as he heard it he slowed his bounding run, let her gently to the ground, only to pick her up by the waist again and turn her round and round like a child. He let her go. They were both laughing, and she was trying to get her breath again.

'Lord Balfour! I have lost my bonnet!'

'Your hair is down. You look so...' Suddenly, he took a step towards her and scooped her up to him, kissing her hair and lips in sudden abandon. Her lips moved beneath his, when he moved to kiss her eyes and face she tilted toward him and made sounds she had never made before. Even as he moved down her slim neck, she leant back to accommodate his insistent mouth, until he kissed the soft ruff at the throat of the dress, and suddenly she grew stiff.

'Sir!' she said, this time in a tone of general outrage. He let her go immediately, the great dark eyes the wounded beast once more. It has only been a few seconds, but it had seemed... She moved briskly to the house, shaken, stirred and humiliated by his behaviour and her own. Never had she been touched in this way, never had she been so wanton, never had she shown herself so without character. She was angry, so angry, too, that he should so use her. She tried to find enough pins in her head to make the simple coil once more, her strands of hair the wreck of her respectability reforming. She entered the house by the side door they had used to exit, and in the hall she met Evans coming from the blue salon.

'Evans, is the dress finished?' She barely had control of her voice.

'No, ma'am. In half an hour or so, miss. I just came to ask if you fancied anything after your walk, miss.' The maid looked a trifle worried at Miss Fleet's change in manner.

'Never mind. Lord Balfour will not mind if I borrow this one. Could you send a footman to look for my cloak and bonnet? I'm afraid I carelessly dropped them and they blew away. Near the sheep's paddock. And have the coachman bring round the horses. I am to set off immediately for Durant. Bring down my bag, please.' Euphemia was used to delivering many orders, some of them awful, to servants for Lady Ellingham. But this was the first time she had ever issued such a string of orders for herself.

'Yes miss,' said Evans stiffly. 'At once!' She took an appraising look at the state of Miss Fleet's hair. Surely it was tidy, but not in the manner she had started the day with. She closed her mouth grimly and mounted the staircase to a footman.

This errand was not necessary, for the slightly dishevelled figure of Lord Balfour had entered, clutching a bent straw bonnet and her cape. The butler relieved him of them and Evans turned at her name, which her master used in a subdued voice. 'Evans, find Miss Fleet another bonnet will you? I appear to have stepped in this one while I searched for it.' Evans curtsied and ran up the stairs.

An interested footman and butler were appearing disinterested at the stiff tableau of Miss Fleet, stock still in the hall, with his Lordship looking supplicating at her.

'Miss Fleet, I—' He stopped. His voice seemed to induce a spasm in her body that she could not disguise. 'Might I ... I ... beg you have a word in the salon?'

Her bosom heaved. It needed only this. 'The *blue* salon?'

'I— no—.' He stopped again, realising his mistake and walked to the larger salon, the butler discreetly opening the door.

Euphemia moved forward to follow him and stopped on the threshold, confronted by the portrait of the beauteous Lady Balfour in the full bloom of her youth. She grasped her hands before her and nearly juddered back when His Lordship came towards her again, but he only moved past to shut the door so that they might not be overheard. She moved to the fireplace, to stand beneath the painting, determined that he might look full in the face the differences he was trying to ignore. She felt tears threaten her, but she was too outraged to let them fall. She lifted her chin and looked at him. He was so penitent looking, but she was not fooled. He had played on her love for wounded animals quite enough.

'I am so sorry, Miss Fleet. I had no intention, none at all, of behaving in such a way.'

'Which way? Lifting me from my feet and running away with me?'

'We were laughing at that.'

'I suppose I was therefore responsible for what happened next?'

'My dear Miss Fleet, I never meant to ... not until I had spoken to you, had asked you to be my wife.'

Miss Fleet, who had thought herself well beyond the age where any hope or faint dream of such a thing as marriage should be offered to her, could never have believed that when it was — and by a handsome baron — her primary emotion would be anger. As it was, anger had featured very little in Miss Fleet's life. But so many feelings were tumbling passionately inside her, and they were erupting as never before.

'You do not want a wife sir, you want a mannequin to animate your dead wife's clothes and sit in her chair and — and — no doubt many other things you miss. You want a clockwork woman.' He grunted and tried to find his voice, but she continued. 'No doubt you think your high standing and good looks should make me grovel at the thought of having such an offer made to me—'

'No, you are wrong—, please, Euphemia! I have frightened you, you who have been so sheltered all your life—'

'I should be honoured to receive any respectable offer of a home and companionship from a decent man. A quiet, contented life. But you offer me so much more. How could I live knowing that when we kissed you were really kissing a *dead woman*?'

She left the room then, and he let her go, great head bent in sadness, perhaps. Her words must have wounded him, she could hardly believe she had uttered them. But she was too angry to care. She escaped to the blue room to compose herself, caressing the white gilded harpsichord with her fingers. She wiped the hot tears when she heard the horses and found Evans awaiting her in the vestibule, bonnet and cape in hand. She put them on dumbly. He did not come to see her off. She could not have faced him, so she was glad. She sat in an old fashioned but luxurious coach, with an unnecessary hot brick for her feet and a fur rug cast over her knees by Tinder himself. He looked full into her eyes when he finished and it seemed as though he would have said something, but did not. He stepped back and Evans handed her night bag, and said, 'Your dress is within, miss. It lacks some stitches yet.'

'Do not worry Evans. I can finish it. And thank you for all your work.'

'It was a pleasure, miss.' She disposed a basket of provisions from cook. 'The master asked that you have these things to lighten the journey miss.'

Miss Fleet, overcome, merely nodded.

'Oh miss,' said Evans, suddenly pleading, 'can you not stay? You do him so much good, my master.'

Miss Fleet could barely speak. 'Thank you Evans. But I cannot!'

Evans shut the door and the coach moved away. Was it really only thirty hours since she had entered this house? The butler raised a sad hand to her. Tinder stood, looking wounded, and Evans beside him, tall as Euphemia had first seen her, but evidently moved. Somehow, she too felt the pain of parting from them. It was hardly credible that she should feel so after this short time, but they had gone through the shadow of death together, and had silently acknowledged, by looks and gestures, their shared fear and relief.

The carriage passed the small sheep paddock.

She could not look.

Chapter Five

Friends Reunited

Arriving at the great estate of Viscount Durant, Euphemia found herself bone weary. She was vaguely aware of a very large and handsome house in some light coloured stone surrounded by beautifully landscaped gardens. Her eyes had shed enough reluctant tears on that journey for a sea, but she had ruthlessly obliterated them when she'd espied the house with the aid of an ill-used handkerchief. She fell out of the carriage and into Felicity's outstretched arms with a plucky smile on her face.

'My dearest Euphemia! How I have missed you.' Felicity was a tall dark beauty, still very young, with the gift for dispensing happiness suggested by her name — even in her darkest days, when Miss Fleet had first met her. She was dressed even more elegantly than when they has last met, as befitted a new viscountess, in a silk day dress of the finest Parisian cut. It was a deeper colour, too, than her maidenhood had allowed, a cherry red that suited her dark beauty particularly well.

Some silk rosebuds had been artfully arranged in her coiffure, and she looked so grown up that Euphemia smiled through her tears.

'Felicity, you look so elegant.'

'My continental polish, Sebastian calls it, and he laughs at me very much. But you too look so very lovely, my dear Euphemia. I am so glad you bought yourself a new bonnet! And such an elegant one.' Miss Fleet had forgotten the bonnet, which she had not even regarded. They were walking through the huge oak door, three times their height, arm-in-arm together, and Euphemia was beginning to calm herself.

'It is mere borrowed finery, my dear. My own bonnet had an accident this morning.'

'Well, come and see Sebastian. He wanted to come out to greet you, but I said I *must* have you for myself at first.'

The relaxed, elegant figure of Viscount Durant came forward to greet her as she entered the salon, and he took both her hands. 'My dear Miss Fleet, Euphemia! Welcome to your new home!' He stood back a little. She still wore her bonnet, but her cape was open and he spied the dress with the yellow primroses. 'I declare you I have never seen you look lovelier!'

Euphemia, who had been shyly smiling at him, suddenly wrenched her hands free. 'Oh, do not say so,' and ran from the room, with Felicity following her, with a confused backward glance at her beloved.

Alone in her lovely room, Miss Fleet looked at herself in the bonnet she had never seen. It was a blue silk poke bonnet, probably chosen by Evans to match her old cloak. The yellow flowers at one side referred to the borrowed dress, too, and she had to admit it suited her. She looked anew. With all the compliments flying, could it really be that she was passably handsome? Is this what clothes did for one, even when one had been crying, or trying to stop crying, for three hours? She did not want to be told she was looking lovely, as he had. She could not bear it. It was all kindness, of course, but she would rather be overlooked than wear things that obliged people to remark. She did not wish to hear any of The Bear's words again. Did he really propose? Was she mad to refuse him? She imagined telling her staid sister that a giant baron had offered for her, and that she had refused him.

If Theodora could even be brought to believe such a thing, she would have her sister sent to a lunatic asylum for the refusal. *No one* could understand. She caught sight of herself again. Was the spirit of Lady Balfour somehow softening the lines of her face (or was that the bounty of the viscount's London home?) and giving her a new elegance? She would put the dress and the bonnet away, after today, and with them all memories of the baron and her own wanton behaviour.

Then perhaps, everything would be the same again. This feeling of being awake after a long sleep watching other people's lives was not comfortable. As she looked out of the window, she saw all things with a new clarity, and an aching sense of connection. It was as though when she had seen such a sylvan scene before, there had been some grey medium between it and her. The cocoon she had spun about herself to stop feeling so much, perhaps. A light had been switched on within her, but with it came the pain. She felt everything too much, she relived each moment with him, not as she remembered Papa and Mama, but in a visceral way. The memory of his loud voice and teasing smile shook her physically. And the waves of heat that took over her whole self when she remembered his kisses was not just humiliation, but something else ... something much stronger. She could not allow herself to think of him, yet the thoughts arose in her and overpowered her. His great mane of hair, those deep dark eyes, his booming laugh. But she would stop it. She would.

At the same time she was worried for his health. She replayed the scene in the salon where they parted and could not remember any rasping in his breathing, not even after her cruel words. She wished she could take them back, but she could not. But he was well, she had to believe it. Perhaps she might write to Tinder or Evans for news. But she was being ridiculous, and she knew it. Baron Balfour was none of her affair, and she would put him away tomorrow with the sprigged muslin gown.

'Well, I cannot account for it, Sebastian,' said Felicity when she had come downstairs after seeing her friend disposed in her bedchamber. Quite naturally, she found herself sitting on his knee, answering his open arms as he lounged in the elegant scroll-ended sofa nearest the fire.

He kissed her soundly before saying, 'I have never known Miss Fleet to display such emotion. Try as I might, I could never get her to be more than a little mouse in my presence.'

'Now she is afraid that you will wish her gone, but I put her mind at rest on that score at least.' As she heard the door opening, she slid from his knee with practised ease and sat beside him. Rutland disposed of the tea tray on a small table which he put near his mistress and she began, in a very wifely way, she thought, to make the tea.

Sebastian grinned, watching her, 'Well, if she becomes a watering pot over dinner...'

'Bastain!' she said, but saw that he was still grinning.

'I must admit, that when you broached the subject of Miss Fleet's coming to stay with us, I had some doubts. But in the weeks she spent with us in London before the wedding trip she was a delight. She had a trick of disappearing suddenly when I wished to kiss my wife...'

'She read your wicked eyes. I know *I* do.'

'But what on earth did I do to upset her?'

'I do not know, she will not tell me. But I think she was overwrought before she came here. The friend of yours whom she visited, he could not have upset her in any way? I think she will tell me all when she is a little rested. She assures me she shall be down for dinner - I adjured her not to change, for I believe she needs the rest.'

'I hardly think that Balfour would have upset her. He is great fellow, who has become something of a recluse after the death of his wife. He is a loud and booming giant of a man and I suppose he might have scared our little mouse somewhat.'

'Oh yes,' said Felicity, 'she does jump at loud voices, like Lady Ellingham's in one of her worse moods. Never mind, we shall make her comfortable again. But I wonder how she knows Lord Balfour?'

At dinner that night, Lord Durant asked this question. Miss Fleet, still dressed in her muslin with primroses, looked as neat as ever, but somehow the face that Bastian had thought a little closed and tight was somewhat softer. She answered quietly, though, and he thought perhaps she had prepared her answer.

'I had a little accident and a chance meeting with Lord Balfour meant that he took me to his home nearby. Then, I am afraid he had an attack—'

'His old trouble, *I see...*' said the viscount.

'And I felt I had to stay until he felt restored.'

'So like you, dear Euphemia. And Lord Balfour is now well?' asked Felicity.

'He was ill for some hours, but the next morning he was quite himself.'

'A loud and booming sort of man, my husband says.'

'Oh yes, the first time I heard his voice I jumped.'

'So would I have, I'm sure. I did when Aunt Ellingham shouted at me.'

'Oh, you were so much braver than I, Felicity.'

'You were both splendidly brave as I remember it, but I will not have that lady's name turn our stomachs at this, your first meal at Durant, Miss Fleet.'

They laughed then, Euphemia shyly behind her napkin, and Felicity was glad to see her look more relaxed. Bastian had a temper, but he had never displayed it since their marriage, and he had always been kinder than his reputation. She had known he would make her friend comfortable.

Felicity genuinely believed that her friend would confide her upset at the outset of her visit. But Euphemia did not. She seemed almost her quiet self, but Felicity noticed a certain unevenness of spirits — despite her friend having herself well in hand. She had, initially, tried to act rather as a poor relation might, running to bring Felicity her shawl, or stooping to pick up her work threads before she had time to retrieve them herself, and Felicity had had to be firm.

'You are not here to be a servant, Euphemia, but part of the family. You must do as you please at all times, and not run after me.'

For the next week, Euphemia dressed again in the brown cambric or the grey poplin that Felicity had seen so often before, the grey with a new paler insert in the bodice that had been necessitated, said Euphemia, by a spill of chocolate. Felicity had seen her working on the bodice, and said. 'Oh that pearl grey damask is very pretty, where had you it from, Euphemia?'

Her friend's face had shut once more and she said merely, 'Oh, I had it given to me.'

'We shall have some dresses made for you now you are here, Burton tells me that there is an excellent woman in the village, a Madame Blanc.'

'Oh, there is no need, my dear,' said Euphemia.

'But Burton says she is a French émigré with six children to feed, so I think it only right that we help her by ordering you some gowns. I, too, will have some made from the fabrics I bought on my wedding trip. But Lady Aurora writes that I must wait until next month when she and Mr Fenton come, so that she can see what I have. Then she will design some dresses for me.'

'Yes, I am so glad that Lady Aurora will finally see you in your home.'

'But in the meantime, my dear Euphemia, Madame's children must eat.'

Euphemia laughed, and Felicity was glad to see it.

'We shall go tomorrow.'

But by tomorrow, there was no need to go to Madame's, for when Felicity and Euphemia returned from their morning walk (while Bastian met with his agent in the library) a large coach was pulled up outside the white columns, and a number of bags and boxes were being unloaded under the eye of a rather terrifying looking servant.

'Evans!' exclaimed Euphemia. Felicity looked down at her friend, but she was already moving off after her shock.

'Isn't that the coach you arrived in, Euphemia? Lord Balfour's?'

'Yes! I—' she answered, but she was near enough to the maid now to talk to her over the welter of servants carrying the packages. Felicity noticed a number of hat boxes among them and wondered. 'Evans,' said Euphemia, a little sharply, 'what is the meaning of this? Lord Balfour is not *here*?'

Evans bobbed a curtsy. 'No miss. His Lordship sent me. He hopes that I may stay a few days to alter the gowns, miss. He sent these.' Evans made her steady way forward and held out two notes, one addressed to the viscount.

'What's this?' said the viscount, coming languidly out of the house to meet them, 'Are the Fentons arrived early? This is a lot of baggage, even for Lady Aurora, unless she's moving in.'

Felicity was watching her friend, who was standing stock still, clutching the letters to her heaving bosom, her cheeks a high colour, obviously trying to repress some powerful emotion. Felicity, in sheer amazement, thought it might be *anger*. 'Is not one of those letters for Bastian, my dear?' she prodded, gently.

Euphemia held it out, dumbly. Obviously still under some pressure of feeling.

The viscount opened it, and read the brief contents. 'Richard wants us to house a maid, so that she can work on these,' he vaguely gestured to the boxes which, mercifully, had reached their end, 'to fit them to Miss Fleet.' He raised his eyebrows at Miss Fleet, still standing stock still, the other letter crumpled in a fist at her side, obviously still trying to control herself, Felicity noted concernedly. 'Yes, you *are* of Lady Balfour's small stature, come to think of it, Miss Fleet. I daresay they will become you well.'

'Oh,' said Felicity, when her friend seemed unable to answer. 'I expect the lovely white and yellow muslin was one you borrowed when you spilt the chocolate on your grey poplin, and he realised—'

'Excuse me,' said Euphemia, evidently barely managing to get out the words, 'I must go—'

'Euphem–!' said Felicity, and would have followed if the viscount had not held her back.

'Let her calm herself a little. Something about this gesture of Balfour's has upset her. He's not known for his subtlety and she may be embarrassed by it.'

'It is very kind of him, but I expect she feels of it as charity, for she does not want even *I* to buy her clothes. *Was* Lady Balfour so like Euphemia?'

'Not at all, except in figure. They were an odd looking pair, a gruff giant and a fairy princess, strangely mated. But they were very happy together. And Lady Balfour had exquisite taste in clothes. Having met Miss Fleet, I expect that Balfour thought that this would be a practical solution as to what to do with his wife's affairs. It seems eminently sensible. Perhaps she feels they are two years out of fashion?'

They had re-entered the house during this conversation, and Felicity sat down on a sofa facing his and laughed. 'She, who has been wearing ten-year-old gowns? I hardly think so.' She stood up again. 'I know you advised me to be patient, but I cannot wait. I'm going to her now to ease her feelings.'

Euphemia was in her chamber when Felicity found her, holding up an exquisite blue muslin gown, with a satin under-dress of the same hue. Felicity held back in the doorway, for the strange, stern maid who had given her friend the letters was talking to her. Felicity knew she was eavesdropping, but it was her house after all, and she felt she needed to do so to understand her friend's evident pain.

'It is quite finished, miss,' the maid was saying. 'I was able to do so because we had not removed the pins. The rest of them will only take a few days to finish, miss, if you will let me measure. And His Lordship also ordered me to make what changes you might like, miss, to adjust them to your taste. Especially the bonnets miss, he asked me to adjust the colour and trims to suit your colouring, miss.'

'They are *her* clothes!' said Euphemia passionately.

'But so very beautiful, miss. And almost made for you. They could be of use to few women else. And my mistress would have been happy to know they were worn — for though generous, waste she could not bear.' She took the blue dress from Euphemia's hands, and said in a gentling tone that is used to sooth infants, 'You did look so lovely in it, miss. And what can it matter to you that they are my lady's attire? You never met her.'

'No,' said Euphemia. 'But I cannot accept them.'

'Then the moth will have them, and that does seem a pity.' Euphemia said nothing, and the maid continued. 'He is so set on this miss, that if I return with the boxes, I believe he might have another attack.' She seemed to be looking at Euphemia closely, 'And I *know* you wouldn't want that.'

'No—' said Euphemia, weakening. Felicity thought it time to intervene.

'I came to see what riches Lord Balfour sent.' She looked at an array of gowns laid across the bed, the chairs, and every other available surface. 'Oh, how fabulous these are. Lady Balfour must have been a London hostess of the first stare,' she said, holding up a cream silk evening gown with one enormous silk rose in the same fabric, under the bodice.

'My lady never visited town,' said Evans quietly.

'Never? Then how came her gowns to be so fashionable?'

'She had the fashion plates from magazines, miss, and she loved to copy and adapt the latest designs. Beautiful things made her happy.'

'Her whole house shows that,' said Euphemia in a removed voice.

'Well, you *will* look lovely in this dress.' Felicity turned to the maid, 'Evans is it? Could you have it ready for tomorrow night? We will have some guests for dinner.'

'It is too fine for me,' said Euphemia flatly.

'Nonsense! You will look quite the thing,' she grasped her friend's hand and sat her on a pile of dresses on the bed, joining her. 'Euphemia, I know that this is an overwhelming gift for such a slight acquaintance, but believe me it makes sense. Why, these gowns might have been made for you, and it would be such a shame to throw them away.'

Euphemia's large eyes looked into Felicity's equally large, and very kind eyes. 'I suppose it would. But bonnets, too!' she said so tragically it almost made Felicity laugh. 'He sent me bonnets!'

Felicity jumped up and looked, taking a green silk from a hat box, saying, 'This must go with that French pelisse. Oh, how smart you will be, Euphemia.'

'I cannot wear such a profusion of flowers.' Euphemia pointed to the pink ribbon flowers tucked inside the brim at one side to add a little dash.

'Why not? The other became you so well.'

'I would look ridiculous, in my position.'

Euphemia's eyes fell and she clutched at her hands, gripping back something. Felicity led her gently up.

'Come, let's walk again, you are a little emotional. Your position is a member of the family in the Viscount Durant's home. How can your dress be too fine? Felicity turned with her customary smile. 'Evans? Please put away the gowns for the present, I believe Miss Fleet to be rather overwhelmed by Lord Balfour's generosity.'

'Very well, Your Ladyship. Perhaps...?' said Evans, holding out a claret merino wool pelisse to Euphemia, 'I think there is a chill in the air, miss.'

Euphemia put it on, as though defeated, and she headed towards the door.

'I have the bonnet for that, miss.'

'My straw will suffice, thank you, Evans.'

She did not speak on her way downstairs and it was not until they arrived at the little bench in the walled garden that was at one side of the house that Felicity said, 'Dearest Euphemia, will you not tell me what occurred to you on your journey to make you so upset? Your letter in response to my invitation was so joyous that I made sure you were looking forward to coming. So it is only your meeting with Lord Balfour that can have upset you so. Sebastian says that he is a giant with no subtlety of manner, and that he may have said something blunt to upset you.'

'I *am* happy to have come here, dear friend. The home you give me here means so much to me —' her voice changed, becoming harder, 'and it gave me the power to refuse Lord Balfour.'

'Lord Balfour *offered* for you?' Felicity was all agog. 'Dearest, did you not think him honourable, or do you dislike him? Had you not just met him?' She realised that she had shot out her questions in a line, and could not expect them to be answered all at once.

'I *had* just met him, but it didn't seem that way...' Euphemia's eyes looked into the distance, remembering. Felicity stirred, suddenly wondering, but stilled herself so as not to break the beginning of the confidences. As she watched her friend, some part of her could not help noticing how well the claret wool pelisse became her, a high curved collar, like gentlemen's shirt points framing her face, drawing attention to her large eyes. It had a double breasted bodice with large blue buttons and navy braiding. Felicity felt a little covetous. 'We spent many hours with each other in the two days, for he needed me to talk — to calm him during an attack. I don't think anyone has wanted me to talk that long in all my life.'

'So he *offered* for you?'

Miss Fleet gave a bitter laugh, a sound that shocked Felicity. Her little friend was *angry*. 'Oh, not for *me*. He offered for a *doll* to wear his beautiful, dead wife's clothes and sit in her sitting room, and walk where they walked together, and, and—' her voice cracked, her rage broke and she sobbed unrestrainedly into her hands.

'Oh come here, my sweet friend,' said Felicity gathering her into her arms. 'He expressed himself badly, I suppose. He is a rough man, perhaps.'

'A *bear*!'

'A bear, yes, but from what Sebastian has said, a good man. Perhaps he wanted contentment in his later life, someone to be his companion and he phrased it wrongly.'

'Oh, he wants no simple companion. I may have been honoured to receive such an offer, might even have accepted such a thing for my own true home and—' she seemed to recollect what she said and looked pleadingly at Felicity. 'You understand that I am not ungrateful—'

'Of course not. I understand completely.'

'He wants more than a mere companion, he wants his beauty back. He wants his love, and he has shown me by putting his hands on me so—!' Her breath caught. 'I cannot *speak* of it.'

Felicity was shocked and alarmed. 'Hush now, my pet. Do not distress yourself. If he treated you disrespectfully, or roughly, if he frightened you, you must put those thoughts away. You are safe now. I can see that Lord Balfour must be less than a gentleman, whatever Sebastian says, to have given you such a disgust of him.'

'Oh, but Felicity, I was not disgusted *at all*.'

Felicity held her, amazed.

Euphemia returned to her room, to lie down before dinner, and to will herself to stop this crying immediately. The viscount must *never* see her so or he would wish for her departure, and rightly so. Years of training deserted her and her feelings were churned about like so much butter. The room was mercifully returned to its normal state,

EUPHEMIA AND THE UNEXPECTED ENCHANT... 49

excepting the blue gown which had been laid out for dinner by Evans. She sat on the bed and picked up the letter he had written, whose seal she had not yet breached. Her hands shook as she opened it.

My dear Miss Fleet,

I have apologised for my behaviour, and I cannot yet explain it, even to myself. To see you laugh, to see you so lovely,

'Lies!' she cried, almost throwing the parchment aside, but she read on...

...standing in front of me like that, I lost my head. There is no excuse. I frightened you, manhandled you, when I should have been begging you respectfully like an honest man, to be my wife. Instead, I shocked and disgusted you. How I wish I could go back to the moment before that, when you were looking at me and laughing, when I should have bent my knee to you, begged you —.

But I did not. I know you are making your home with Sebastian, and I hope that sometime in the future we might meet again as friends, at least.

'I will be far from here if ever I know you are coming. I shall *never* see you again!' Euphemia cried it aloud.

...It was not her dresses that made me wish you to stay with me, you know. At first, I admit you were so like in size that you brought her back to me a little. To see you, so small and neat among her things brought me joy. But it was yourself that drew me further, Miss Fleet. You must know that to be so.

'If only that were so,' Euphemia cried aloud, as though to Lord Balfour himself. She stood and regarded herself in the mirror. Something had happened to her face, she knew not what, it looked somehow different, but her hair was still a shade of brown called mouse, her lips thin and nose nothing at all. She could not compare to the ravishing beauty of the portrait. She would be found wanting by him every day of her life. 'I do not know it.' she said as she turned back to the paper, addressing Lord Balfour again.

...Do not think that my sending the gowns is an attempt to woo you. I know, if anything, that it may make you angrier at me. But, dear lady, I am letting go of them to their new home. Who else can they be of use to? And though I dreaded that you would be offended, I thought too that you, who have had so little given to you in this life, might find some joy in wearing gowns that better display the lady you are...

'No, the *other* lady that you *wish* me to be!'

... and that you would feel more at home in those grand surroundings, already dressed for the part. I know your sensitivity makes you feel yourself a mere pensioner, not realising what you give to those around you. You melted the frozen heart of Evans, and the jealousy of Tinder. In such a short time, you cast a balm upon this place.

Please, my dear Miss Fleet, do me the infinite honour of accepting my gift, knowing, as you do, that it cost me nothing at all. I wish that you had stayed at Balfour Court and I could have bought you brand new gowns of your own, not stained for you by any other feeling. But my boorish behaviour has undone my hopes. You are like a shy fawn and I would have been better to gentle you, instead I hurt you...

'But not in the way you believe!' she told him.

...My every hope is for your health and happiness, my dear.
If we should not meet again, please know I will never forget you.
Your humble servant,
Richard Audley, Baron Balfour.

Never had Euphemia received such a letter. It had been her dream to own just a few love lines from any man who had shown her partiality. But there had been none. A quiet life in the country with her stern vicar father, a short time in town with her sister, then ten whole years with Lady Ellingham, barely introduced to anyone (since she was of no importance). No one noticed her. No one had ever made her so angry as he. She did not believe she'd *possessed* such anger. Last year she'd been angry for Felicity of course, for the dark aspersions cast on the name of the sweetest friend in the world. But for herself, never. She had acceded to her lot with hardly a whimper, accepting it as her due. She was now being offered the moon and stars, a home of her own and a grand position, and she could not take it. How could she? Eventually, he would be bitterly disappointed. He would see her clearly, and not those things he'd recognised from another. And he would be broken-hearted anew.

She put the letter to her heart and threw herself passionately onto the bed, all hope of discipline thrown to the winds.

Chapter Six

Another Garden Encounter

The viscount entered his wife's dressing room as she stood before the glass, adjusting the neckline of a ravishing gold silk gown, and made his languid way towards her. His wife was not deceived by his languor however, and nodded away her maid. He kissed her neck and shoulders and she leaned back into him so that he grasped her waist firmly. 'No, my dear. We will be late for dinner!'

'When will you learn, my love that dinner in a viscount's house begins only when the viscount appears?'

'Well, it is very unkind to cook, who is trying out a new recipe I brought from France of soufflé. It will collapse, and if it does, so will poor cook.'

'As usual, I am astounded at your knowledge of the servants' feelings, as well as deeply uncaring of same.'

'If I believed that, Bastian, I should leave you for a Captain of the Guards. But I know you sent your valet back to bed today when he was suffering from a head cold.'

'Only because I did not wish to be infected.'

'Your old nurse, when I visited her in her cottage, said that you had never been sick a day in your life!'

'Because I take *precautions*.'

She turned and he kissed her, and for a moment, it seemed that the soufflé must fall. But Felicity looked worried, and pulled away. 'I am concerned about Euphemia.'

'Mmm?' said Bastian, kissing her neck.

'Bastian!' he pulled away and looked at her. 'Things are different than we thought. Lord Balfour has *offered* for Euphemia.'

'Richard? And she refused him?'

'Yes. And the tragedy is, I think she really cares for him.'

'I would say they did not have much time to know their feelings, but I knew how I felt about *you* from the very first.'

'Nonsense! Your only thought was that I was the same height and age as Lady Letitia.'

'Well, perhaps not from the *very* first. But *soon*.' He teased and kissed her again. 'Anyway, if she likes him, why didn't she say yes?'

'It is all wrapped up in those gowns he sent. She is very like Lady Balfour in stature, and she had need of a gown because there was an accident when he shouted—'

'He does that!'

'Yes, well, it was in the inn taproom, where they met, she spilt chocolate on her gown and then he fairly ordered her into his carriage—' Felicity continued.

'Now what kind of gentleman treats a lady like that?' said Durant, shocked.

She regarded him narrowly, knowing he referred to their own first meeting. 'No kind of gentleman at all,' she said, and he laughed. She continued, 'So he took her to Balfour Court, to his wife's own sitting room, and sent her to change her gown for one of Her Ladyship's, and then when he saw her, he had an attack of *asthma* I think she named it, and so then she knew he was using her to bring back the *ghost of his wife*.' Felicity finally took a breath and shuddered dramatically.

'Sounds like one of those ghastly novels you two are so fond of.'

'Yes, but this was *real*. And then when he was so ill — the malady disturbs his breathing, you know — he wanted her to sit and talk to him to calm him, and the servants said he must not be crossed, for it would make him worse...'

'That is true — any agitation inflames the lungs, I have seen it happen.'

'Well, she was in the shocking position of sitting at the bedside of a gentleman she hardly knew—'

'Wicked old Balfour, I didn't know he had that in him.'

'I know you are joking, but do not, my love. Apparently, that strange servant, who was also devoted to Lady Balfour, sat in the room with her the whole time.'

'No damaged reputation, then?'

'Yes, but the next day he was quite well and they went for a walk, and I'm not sure what happened, but he overturned her and ran off with her or something — she was crying and I didn't quite understand what she was saying — and then he caught her in his arms and *kissed* her. Quite roughly, I believe.'

'Well, upon my soul!' despite himself, Durant was nearly as surprised as his viscountess. 'She must have been terrified, poor timid little Miss Fleet.'

'That is just it, Bastian. She *liked* it!'

'I do not understand. Why then did she refuse him?'

'She fears that she can never match to the beauty of his dead wife. That he will be forever searching for something within her that he can never possess. She could have said yes if she did not love him so.' A tear fell from his lovely wife's eyes, but Bastian was frowning.

'What gave her that idea?' he said. 'Oh, I know. That dashed portrait. The gowns!' He turned to leave the room. 'George!' he said to a footman as he headed away from the stairs, and along to another chamber. 'Tell cook to delay the soufflés until I arrive.'

George took this blandly, but departed a broken man.

'What are you doing, my love?' said Felicity following him.

'Correcting a misunderstanding, my sweet.' He stopped and shooed her away as he did his dog. 'I can manage this better on my own, I think.'

She turned and looked at him over her shoulder, her glossy ringlets dancing, 'I will not be your dog, my lord. I'll have you know I'm a viscountess now, and I expect to be treated so.' She moved in a very stately way downstairs, and His Lordship grinned. Then he turned and knocked on Miss Fleet's door, only for it to be opened by the dragon-maid, Evans. 'Is Miss Fleet yet dressed?' he enquired.

'Yes sir. She is about to go to dinner.'

'Viscount?' Miss Fleet called, and appeared on the doorway.

'I require a word with you, Miss Fleet. Can you send your maid away?'

Alarmingly, Evans stood her ground.

'Please leave us, Evans.'

'Yes, miss. If you say so.'

Now that the viscount was in, he seemed to have lost his *sangfroid*. How to begin?

'My lord?' Miss Fleet was enquiring, timidly.

The viscount properly looked at her. She was wearing a blue muslin dress and she looked a little regal. Her hair was arranged somehow differently, and it drew attention to her fine eyes. 'On risk of making you upset again, my dear Miss Fleet, you look quite lovely in that gown.' She blushed. 'Not a good way to start when I have just asked your maid to leave your bedchamber,' he said reflectively, almost to himself. But she smiled shyly. 'Miss Fleet, I came here to talk to you since it appears you are under a misunderstanding about Lady Balfour.'

She stiffened.

'Lady Balfour, Miss Eversham that was, was indeed the belle of the county, I believe, though it was before my time. She had a season in London, where Lord Balfour met her. But she was already engaged to someone else.' Miss Fleet sat down heavily on the bed, and the viscount drew a chair near to it. 'One day, as she walked to the park, she fell under some horses.'

Euphemia gasped.

'Many bones were broken, and some eventually healed – though she had some pain in walking too far. But those on her face did not heal well. I'm afraid a doctor made an ill attempt at setting the bones, and she was terribly disfigured. She looked, ever after, like a cracked-mirror figure of herself. Her jaw bone and cheek bone were mismatched on one side, and her eye drooped from her socket. Her suitor left her, and Lord Balfour offered for her. She sent him away, time and again, afraid to see anyone. But he came, he looked at her, and asked her again. She said yes. I believed they were devoted to each other, and Lady Balfour made Balfour Court into a beautiful home. I knew her as a child, and accepted as all children do, whatever they see. I only knew she was kind to me. She therefore let me visit as an adult, and I was very happy to do so. She never visited London again, had high hedges built so that she could walk on the estate unnoticed. Balfour managed to go to town sometimes, and to visit friends. But mostly he stayed at Balfour Court, though she could never have asked it of him.' He stood up. 'There. I have righted a false impression. Dinner will await you, dear Miss Fleet.' He looked at her returning colour and held out his arm. 'Or are you ready now?'

She took it and glided alongside him, trying to work out what, if anything, this changed.

She was not much use as a raconteur at dinner. She hardly spoke at all. Eventually both the viscount and Felicity stopped trying to draw her out, and left her to her pondering.

Later, when Evans was unpinning her hair, Euphemia asked her, 'Lady Balfour was very beautiful, was she not?'

Evans stopped for a second, then continued, 'My master told her so every day, miss.'

'Yes, yes I see, Evans.' She met the maid's eye in the glass, 'And in your view, Evans?'

'My mistress was as kind and beautiful a lady as ever lived, miss.'

Euphemia's eyes shone. 'I'm sure she was, Evans.'

Evans continued with the unpinning and then said, gently, 'Just, as in a different way, you are, miss.'

Perhaps a tear fell. It was difficult to say, for Evans was lifting the blue dress over Euphemia's head.

Miss Fleet twisted and turned in her bed that night. It did not matter, did it? Whether Lady Balfour was beautiful in the eyes of the world or damaged. *She* was who the baron wanted, not Euphemia. Or only as a dressing doll. Yet it *did* somehow make a difference. First, in showing that his kindness was real, that his character was truly noble. But she had always intuited that. How come she to know him so well in so short an acquaintance? Well, he had been open with her, and encouraged her to share her story. Who in all these years, besides

Felicity, had been interested? But he had been. She had known it from the nature of the scant remarks he had been able to make as he lay there, at the way he opened his eyes at some points, to let her see that he understood the pain and struggle she did not mention. Yes, he was a kind man and a sensitive one, behind his bear-like clumsiness of expression sometimes. And when they talked and walked the next day they had been so comfortable together. There was so much laughter, too. Until... She would not think of that.

She sat up and lit a candle and read his letter for the fifth time. He did not say why he wished to marry her. He did not say he loved ... because he could not lie.

She felt again herself in his arms, his mouth on hers — and it was as though it was still happening, a course of heat moved through her body. For once in her life, whatever his motive, a man had been inclined to her. A good man.

But then there was the shame of her response to him, of letting him glimpse her own desperation to — she hardly knew what. But she cast her head in her hands with humiliation.

She understood now that moral fibre, developed over years, could be crushed in a second by passion. Had she not believed him to be kissing another woman, would she ever have resisted him? The feelings he had let loose in her were so strong. Passion, she supposed. She had read of it in books, and now she felt such a physical yearning to be near him that she could almost ride bareback in her nightdress to find him.

'*Euphemia,*' she said to herself sternly, '*Control yourself.*' But it seemed a vain command.

In the day came Evans, ready to pin some dresses on her even before breakfast. After submitting to this for a half hour, she went downstairs and told Felicity so. The young viscountess said, 'Let us devote the day to it. I'm gasping to explore all those lovely things. I'll come to your room, and I'll bring the gift we brought you from Rome. In all this excitement, I have forgotten it.'

So it was that the day was spent trying on gowns and being pinned into them. Felicity's eagle eye had been trained by Lady Aurora's exceptional taste, and she was occasionally able to suggest a change of ribbon trim on a sash to reflect the colour of Euphemia's eyes, or contrast better to her hair. Euphemia herself was amazed at how changed she seemed in each dress. It was almost that a shade of moods could be created by fabrics.

'It is certainly the case that these might have been made for you, Euphemia. So little alteration necessary. You looked so radiant in the green. I have never seen you in green before.' She realised that the constant praise seemed to upset her friend, unused to compliments as she had always been, so she said. 'Let us to the bonnets.'

There were ten of these, two that Felicity declared a little *démodée* and needed to be remodelled in a more modern style. Evans took careful notes. Euphemia's input was constantly for simplification, removal of flowers or a feather. But once the bonnets were on her, she was overruled, both by Felicity and the looking glass. The bonnets transformed her into another woman, someone à la mode, stylish and very nearly (and this was quite ridiculous) *handsome*. She began to enjoy herself a little. Evans packed up each gown and took a number of them to the sewing room, the first being tonight's cream silk.

'You may wear it with this, my dear,' she said, and pressed a box into her hands. It was lined in satin and contained a ruby pendant, small but with an Italianate setting that Miss Fleet really was enchanted by.

'Oh, Felicity!'

'Sebastian found it. It is quite old, you know. Perhaps a love gift for a lady from two centuries ago. We thought you would like it. You could wear it this evening with the lovely silk gown.'

Euphemia wore the yellow-sprigged muslin once more, and Felicity could not help saying, 'Oh, you look such a *fashionable* little thing! *What* would Lady Ellingham think if she could see you now? I do think Evans has a way with your hair. Let us leave off caps today and walk like wild things with our hats off.'

They went companionably down the stairs arm-in-arm, then, as they reached the hall, they heard a carriage draw up outside.

'Bastian,' Felicity called, 'I believe it is your guest arrived early! We shall have our walk nevertheless, my dear' she added to Miss Fleet. 'Let us go through a side door, to avoid being seen.'

They did so, and the day was fine enough to permit the short wild walk that Felicity suggested, and they moved to the walled garden, which, vast as it was, still provided enough shelter from the wind to feel that you were in an interior space. The peach trees trained on the walls had shed their fruit, of course, but there were still some apples and plums to be had. The little paths between vegetable beds were like a map of miniature city streets, and the ladies wandered around them, meeting an old gardener with a sackcloth apron tending some cabbages. 'Oh Grimes!' Felicity said, 'How splendid all this looks. But I need to talk to you about the roses in the bed near the house. Come with me.' Felicity said, 'Stay here, Euphemia, I will be back in but a moment!' The viscountess got to the door in the wall of the garden, peered through it, looked back at her friend, and said, 'I'm sorry, my dear!'

Euphemia was only confused for a second before the terrible betrayal occurred to her, and that, even before Felicity had disappeared with the gardener, and the huge figure replaced them in the doorway.

'*You!*'

He lurched towards her, and she stepped back, almost overturning herself as her foot hit soft earth rather than path. He was with her

EUPHEMIA AND THE UNEXPECTED ENCHANT...

in two bounds, righting her, and then he stepped back a huge step, giving her space. If only he had not touched her, she might have been stronger, but that searing touch on her arms made her tremble. If only he did not look so apologetic, so worried, so hesitant, so just like the wounded bear, she could tell him to go. But she was silent.

'Durant wrote to me last night. He seemed to think you more than angry, Miss Fleet. He thought you —' he hesitated, '— unhappy.' She just looked at him. 'He said he told you something of my life with my lady. Will you let me explain more?'

She nodded, still looking into the big wounded eyes, hardly daring to breath.

'Let us sit, you will get a crick in your neck looking at me.' He moved towards a stone bench and Miss Fleet found herself remarking, 'I will still get a crick in my neck.'

He laughed shortly. 'Then you stand and I will sit and you will judge the truth in my eyes. I could think of a better arrangement, but—'

Suddenly, Euphemia imagined herself sitting on his knee to better look in his eyes, and blushed. 'Are you quite well, sir?'

'Quite well. The dashed condition comes and goes, often for months at a time, and I am more often well than not. My father had it, and died young. My uncle too, and he still lives at eighty. I feel you should know that. Had I died young, the entailed property and barony would have passed to my brother of course, but there would have been enough, would still be enough, to keep my widow in comfort.'

She swallowed and nodded, and he sat on the bench as she stood facing him, almost eye-to-eye. He began.

'My lady was so badly damaged by the accident, you see, that she did not want to see anyone but a very few friends. We lived perfectly contentedly together, she was a talented and beautiful lady that I was proud to call my wife. She reigned in her little kingdom like the queen she was, but never ventured further.'

'You loved her, but it must have been difficult for you.' She longed to caress his big broad face, and smooth away the pain she saw there, but she was still.

'No, I was happy. I had only to look at some of the bargains my friends had made as a wife,' he growled a laugh, 'and I knew myself to be fortunate indeed.'

'You had no children…?' Euphemia was leading him to answer one of the night-time questions that had so robbed her of sleep.

He sighed, but did not break contact with her eyes. 'This is the delicate thing to say to you, my dear. My wife was fragile. Her face could hardly be borne to be touched and my big monster of a body could never bear to … press upon her … her limbs.'

Miss Fleet gasped and blushed. But she, too, did not look away.

'So when you said I was kissing another, it was never true. And I could hardly believe what I was doing, I am such an *animal*! You, too, are fragile, and I let my passion for you overwhelm—'

He stopped, for Miss Fleet was now on one large knee, her legs dangling between his, her little arms around his huge neck, looking him straight in the eye. 'I am *strong*, not fragile,' she said firmly. He too gasped, and was kissing her in a moment, not gently at all, but fiercely and ravenously. She threaded her fingers through his wiry mane and drew him closer. 'Oh, my love, my love,' he finally whispered at her throat. 'You have bewitched me.'

She kissed his eyes and his wet cheeks and moved towards his lips once more, her body inclining into him, but he took her by the waist, as he had before, and lifted her away from him, and set her firmly on the ground.

'We must not kiss again right now.' He saw he had wounded her again, 'I could eat you whole, with a spoon, my love,' he said, lone large finger tracing her cheek, 'but I will not dishonour you so. Let us walk a little and talk of our wedding.'

'I seem to be inclined to be a fallen woman,' said Miss Fleet, wonderingly, walking by his side once more. 'How *loose* you must think me. But I have never loved before, you see, and I do not seem to be able to temper my feelings.'

His great booming laugh rang out, 'I hope you never do.'

'I did not know myself capable of so much *passion*.'

'I did, when you told me the story of Ellena and that idiot Vivaldi, with such animation and ghoulish intensity. And then you laughed so much when I ran with you in the garden. You were so light and full of joy, I could not stop myself.'

'I never was so before, a big wounded bear of a man brought that out in me.' She held on to his arm and skipped a little to keep up. 'I hope ... I believe...' she said tentatively, blushing as she did so, 'that when one wishes to marry quickly ...?' He looked down at her, with a slightly perplexed look. 'Is it possible, sir...' she said dancing ahead of him and turning towards him, looking up into his eyes, '... that you might procure a special licence?' He picked her up then, and whirled her around, his great booming laugh mingling with hers.

Felicity was in her bedchamber, and alerted by the laugh, which she was surprised did not shake the windows, looked down into the walled garden and wept for joy. 'Oh Bastian! Look!' she said, as he was behind her. He joined her and watched as his friend Balfour shook poor Miss Fleet's bones by spinning her around. By the tinkling laugh they could just hear below the boom, she seemed to be enjoying it.

'Well,' remarked the viscount, 'it looks like you've lost your companion, my dear.'

She turned in his arms, 'And who would have thought that the Viscount of Durant would play Cupid?'

As the baron set her down and bent towards his Euphemia, he stroked her face gently with his great paw, 'Euphemia is such a mouthful, my love. You will be just my Fawn to me.'

'And you, sir,' she said, equally tenderly, 'will always be my Bear.'

Chapter Seven

Epilogue

'Oh, Bastian,' said Felicity reading a letter over the breakfast table, 'Richard and Euphemia are back from their wedding trip and will pay us a visit next week.'

'Excellent!' said her husband, still reading *The Sporting Magazine*.

Lady Aurora Fenton, the most elegant lady in London, and a mother figure to the viscountess, said, 'How long was her trip, my dear?'

'Near four months now,' said Felicity, still reading.

'It must be pleasant for Balfour to be able to travel with this wife, since his first stayed so much at home,' said Mr Wilbert Fenton, equally elegant, if a little florid in dress around the waistcoat area. He was fond of Miss Fleet, who had risked much to help them find Felicity when she had left them last year. Though that had turned out not to be necessary. 'And I love to think of Miss Fleet discovering the world, after the life she's had.' Though he drawled, as usual, he sounded sincere.

Bastian was reading his journal. 'I told you so, sir!' he said, addressing Mr Fenton, '*Fighting Nancy* came in at 20-1!'

'Well, it is lucky that I put a monkey on it.' Wilbert Fenton said, coolly.

'How much is that, pray?' asked the innocent young viscountess.

'Five hundred pounds,' the others chanted, gamblers all, and Felicity smiled.

'Such an amount. Do gentlemen always bet such large sums?'

'Frequently,' said Lady Aurora sadly.

'It amazes me,' said Mr Fenton, crossing his legs, 'that now that I do not need the money, I never seem to lose. It becomes tedious.'

'I know Richard a little,' said Lady Aurora, reminiscently, buttering a hot roll. 'When I was finished being afraid of him, I liked him very well. He has such an imposing presence. I was very sad to hear of his first wife's death, for he mentioned her fondly. It is wonderful to think that he will have a sensible companion like Miss Fleet to spend his quiet life with.'

'Well, from the tone of this letter, they hardly seem to be living a quiet life. Climbing mountains inhabited by bandits in Spain, only to view a little church she wished to see. It sounds so exciting. She writes:

I was always so afraid of life, my dear Felicity, but I cannot be afraid of anything now as long as The Bear is by my side!

...That's what she calls him, isn't it romantic?' said Felicity, with shining eyes.

'And what animal might I be to *you*, my love?' enquired Durant with a heavy sarcasm.

Mr Wilbert Fenton looked up. 'I see you as a kitten, myself.' He lifted his journal to avoid the well-lobbed roll Durant threw at him.

EUPHEMIA AND THE UNEXPECTED ENCHANT...

Felicity laughed, and continued to read, 'Balfour saw off three banditos on his own, Euphemia says — and *she* was obliged to hit one on the head with a stout branch.'

'Well done, Miss Fleet!' said Lady Aurora, laughing.

'The new Lady Balfour is a different creature than we believed, it seems,' said Mr Fenton.

Felicity had continued to read. 'Oh!' she said, shocked, turning her face to her husband's. He twitched the sheet from her hand and she pointed to a line.

'Well,' said Durant, smiling broadly, 'we must cast aside your vision of quiet companionship in the sunset of Balfour's life, Lady Aurora.' She raised her humorous brows in enquiry. 'Lady Balfour is in an interesting condition, with offspring due in five months' time!'

'A cub!' said Lady Aurora, amazed.

'That was quick!' said Mr Fenton. 'Let's hope The Bear was very gentle with our poor Miss Fleet.'

'Oh,' said Felicity with merry eyes, taking a sip of her chocolate, 'I don't think she'd like that at *all*!'

'Well,' said Lady Aurora, summing it up for them all. 'What an *unexpected* enchantment.'

Chapter Eight

Eloise and the Gift of Enthusiasm

The tearoom was full at this hour, it was a large bright space, broken by an elegant stairway that led to a mezzanine floor of extra seating. It would have better suited Oscar Devlin to be seated at the mezzanine table, with the option of overseeing the throng, rather than his prominent position at a table by the window being himself on show, but ...! There were a series of tall window frames overlooking the broad, elegant street, with twenty panes of glass in each, four across and five down — he knew because in his boredom he had counted them. He stretched one long leg out and leaned back in his seat. What was he doing here?

An excited voice reminded him.

'Oh, isn't she *lovely!*'

Two females had pushed through the gap between the window tables, and stood, huddled together, gazing at the street through the tall window nearest Devlin.

'We should go back, Eloise!' said one in an anxious voice.

'In a moment. We must watch how she *captures the lash*, Jenny!'

Oscar Devlin was engaged in so doing also. The lady who had driven the phaeton here herself was slim, blonde, dressed in a pelisse that hugged her upper form, in forest green twill with turquoise military frogging, and a tall collar of turquoise velvet. She had pulled up her phaeton outside the tearoom and as she caught the lash elegantly, her groom rushed to the horses' heads. She tied off the reins, then four helping hands, all from gentlemen gathered in the street, were offered to her. Instead of accepting these gentlemen, she leapt down with the help of a tiger, and was obscured from view by the surrounding gentlemen. Another female was there, but no one offered help to the maid in the cape and she leapt down and followed her mistress through the throng and into the tearoom.

This was the renowned Miss Ottley. In case he should miss anything of interest about that young lady, the chattering female to his side kept a commentary. 'Do you know that she is the only female in Harrogate who drives a high perch phaeton? I should be *terrified*, but Miss Ottley is so proficient as to cast the most fashionable of *gentlemen* into the shade. How elegant she is, and graceful. Can you imagine me jumping from the perch unaided?'

'Even aided you would end in the mud. Let us go back, Eloise,' said the practical, slightly anxious voice of the enthusiast's friend.

'Oh, but *where* did she get that pelisse? That collar height would knock off my bonnet, I expect, but Miss Ottley has such a long, elegant neck. I saw her at a musical evening last week and I swear her skin is as flawless as a babe's. If *I* were to wear that bonnet, with no poke, my freckles would join up. They did so one summer, and Jeffrey said that it looked as though there was a map of Northumberland on my nose.'

Devlin, who had sat cloaked in his private misery, almost choked at this, and took the glance to the side that he had forbidden himself as inquisitive and almost as bad manners as the young spectators displayed. He just saw a red spiral curl or two at her neck, below her bonnet and above a mustard pelisse, and he understood the allusion to freckles. He pitied the poor friend, who was trying to return Miss Ottley's devotee to the respectability of her seat.

'Oh, she's *coming*!' said the enthusiast, almost squeaking in excitement. 'I have heard that she comes here each week to meet with her old governess. Is that not *kindness* itself?'

'Come and sit, Eloise dear. It is not polite to stare so.'

'I know Jenny, but amid all the *other* stares, *mine* will not be noticed. Did you see her catch the lash with such finesse?' The two girls had turned, and one hand of the mustard pelisse flew in the air in imitation, perhaps, of Miss Ottley's elegant catch of the whip's lash. Unfortunately, it hit a dowager's bonnet and an ornamental cherry flew off. The mustard pelisse bent to retrieve it from the floor, full of apologies. The dowager (for so he believed her to be since in the minutes of his boredom he had heard her addressed as Lady Tyler, and so too had a thin, scared looking individual beside her), was mortified. She grasped the cherry and told the curtsying girl to take herself *owrff* immediately.

Miss Ottley had entered the tea rooms and joined an older, plainly dressed dame at a seat in a corner, causing her unrequested entourage of gentlemen to find themselves places to sit — her maid retreating to a servants' bench beneath the stairs.

'Here!' one man called to a waitress, 'Whose parcels are these? I wish to sit.'

Devlin spared a glance at this rudesby and found him to be a flashily dressed man in a striped waistcoat that alone, Devlin considered, would be enough to have him blackballed from Watier's, Devlin's London club. The friend of the young lady from the window tripped forward and said, 'They are mine, Mr Prince.'

'Yours?' the young man said with derision. 'Then remove them.'

Devlin was leaving, having achieved his goal, but he moved to the table, the little redhead behind him. 'I believe this table is occupied,' he said to the man who was looking aggressively at a pale little lady bending to retrieve the parcels.

'And *who* are *you*?' the man's voice was loud enough to draw the attention of adjoining tables.

'Someone with manners,' replied Devlin briefly. He nodded to the females, 'Do be seated, ladies.' The two schoolgirls, for they seemed not much more, sat. One was pale and anxious, one was flushed, but with excitement, not embarrassment. The freckles across her nose might make a map indeed, Devlin reflected. Green eyes looked up at him with merry gratitude. She was, he reflected, an imp.

The aggressive gentleman, finally taking in the cut of Devlin's coat, moved off.

'Thank you, indeed, sir!' said the redhead cheerily.

Devlin's face was neutral as he bowed. He was astonished to be *touched* as he turned away. He turned back to the freckled face who leant towards him and said in a whisper, 'Isn't she *lovely?* Did *you* come to see her, too?'

He disengaged his arm, and making no reply he looked at her coldly, while she ... *winked!* He moved off stiffly, sorry that his manners had insisted that he intervene.

As Devlin left the tearoom he was accosted by the flashy waistcoat, accompanied by a blushing man in an ill-fitting coat. 'Excuse me, my lord,' the man said in an insinuating manner.

'I do not know you sir, kindly let me pass.' Devlin's tone was icily repressive.

'I know *you*, however. Horace here says you are Viscount Devlin. I was sorry to upset you, but do you know who those *ladies*,' here he spoke with heavy irony, 'are? They are merely girls from the Academy. No one of importance at all.'

Devlin was bored and showed it.

'Hansard's academy, you know. Where tradespeople send their offspring to gain manners above their station. You need not have put yourself out for such as they.'

Devlin stared hard at the young man, but he was imperturbable. It was his friend ... Horace, was it? ... who pulled on his elbow in an embarrassed fashion and let Devlin pass.

Why had he come to such a god-forsaken place? He had seen Miss Ottley, at least. She looked, he thought miserably, just as she had been described. Beauty and elegance were there, and the driving suggested skill as well as courage. He had yet to see about intelligence. She must be considered kind to meet with her governess, the redhead suggested.

But Suzanna Caldicott should be Viscountess Devlin, and the future Duchess of Radcliffe, not anyone else. It was too soon, he thought, too soon. But he understood his father, they had seen how unpredictable the world could be, and now he wished to secure Devlin's future, and the future of his line.

This was to assume that Miss Ottley, famed in Harrogate at least, and soon, surely, in London, would accept his offer. She had obviously, after all, any number of suitors. He supposed he might become preferred to the flashy waistcoat, but it was quite possible that she had formed some other attachment or inclination. Even as Devlin hoped so, he knew it was nothing to be relieved about. If it was not to be Miss Ottley, it would be some other with perfect lineage, and perhaps less beauty and accomplishments, who would become his betrothed.

He would attend the Assembly Rooms at least, he resolved, and dance with her once or twice, to see if he could bear it.

***

Devlin was at the side of the ballroom, overlooking Miss Ottley's court, who were positioned at the other side. He had seldom seen such universal admiration, even in a London ballroom, Miss Ottley's admirers standing two deep around her. He watched as she dealt with this: she smiled a little but was reserved too. She was not flirtatious, that he could see from this distance, but neither was she overly proud. Her manner could be described as friendly, but not encouraging. Her mother (or was it chaperone?) should work harder to break up the throng, he thought. It must be somewhat oppressive.

Something drew his attention to the tall double doors of the assembly rooms. It was the red hair. She entered behind an older lady and gentleman and looked around her at the chandeliers, and the tall space with gilt edged wall panels and copious flower stands, with awe. She lifted her head left and right and ended by whirling around, as though in a dance of ecstasy. She bumped into an elderly lady as she did so and knocked her fan to the floor. The lady in front obviously called on her and there was the whole curtsying of regrets and apologies, she bent to retrieve the fan and knocked heads with a lackey who was doing the same, and so she *curtsied at the lackey,* and Devlin heard a vulgar snort emerge from his mouth. Her self-description was not untrue. She was like a carthorse let loose in a porcelain workshop. Her first assembly in these rooms, he concluded. And a dreadful start.

Devlin took his eyes from the scene at last and strolled to ask the master of ceremonies to introduce him to Miss Ottley. This gentleman was happy to serve such an exalted guest and so Devlin had his dance with her, beating some rivals who sent him looks of dislike. She seemed happy enough to partner him, but was not overawed by it, even though the master had described him as Viscount Devlin, heir to the Duke of Radcliffe. There had been a brief spark of satisfaction in her eyes, at first, but she had reverted to mere politeness. That she valued herself to this extent was attractive to him, he thought. She knew how to conduct herself, at least.

This assembly was a less elite affair than those he attended in London, with the upper class, the professions, and the rich in trade all in attendance. Here and there was behaviour that appeared crude and a trifle unruly. In particular, these Northerners seemed to act with more familiarity than he found pleasing or polite. The lower sort of manners seemed to affect even the provincial aristocracy: couples hung from each other's arms, people talked and slapped shoulders, or greeted each other with outstretched hands. He overheard some ribald jokes, too, from groups of gentlemen, words that should not be spoken in the presence, however distant, of ladies. Miss Ottley was above all this, at least.

She danced with elegance and exchanged some cool looks with him, her head tilted upwards to give him a view of her perfect jawline. She was really very beautiful. He could imagine that face and figure, dressed more richly than now, rendered in a painting that would grace his ancestral walls. If one had to look at one face over breakfast each morning, he considered, it might as well be one as aesthetically pleasing as Miss Ottley's.

At the end of the dance, she gave him a warm look, and her hand squeezed his supporting arm a little before he left her with her parents.

It was encouragement of a sort, he supposed, and she smiled at him shyly as he left.

Unexpectedly, this encouragement had dis-encouraged him, he could not think why. Perhaps that her admirable detachment had been broken. His eye moved around the room again as he thought this, and he witnessed the antithesis of detachment.

The crazy tight spirals of red hair that framed her face and hung from her top knot drew his eye again. She grasped at a gentleman's arm from behind and led him to a seat. It was against good form once more. The grey-haired man, very elderly, cupped his hand over the one on his arm, and she chatted with him eagerly. A younger gentleman asked her to dance, he believed. She smilingly shook her head. Devlin thought she indicated the old gentleman as her swain, since the old man laughed as she gestured to him. They were joined by two old dames of the middle class, he assumed by the simpler style of their caps, and the redhead seemed to be their delight.

The difference in dress was quite obvious, Devlin considered. the redhead was dressed prettily in French muslin. He was rather an expert in woman's attire, for reasons that young ladies of virtue would never discover. Her muslin was fine, and expensive, even if simple. The elderly gentleman with her belonged to the professional class at one time, the viscount considered. A physician, a lawyer or some such. Worthy and respectable, but it was unlike fashionable young ladies to keep company with such people at a ball. Eventually, she stood, and with a friendly wave to each she tripped off.

As his eye followed her, someone was talking to him, and he answered at random.

The girl gazed around the room, searching perhaps for her party, and accidentally met his eye, although fifteen feet separated them. Her finger jerked to point, in a manner not particularly mentioned in the book of young ladies' etiquette, towards the left side of the room. His eye followed her finger to Miss Ottley's general location. He looked back. She smiled at him, encouragingly, he thought, and made a gesture that might have been in imitation of her idol catching the lash. As always, the attempt rebounded on her: this time the decorative fan hanging from her wrist slapped a neighbouring lady on the arm. As she turned to apologise, the repressed laugh rose in him again.

Someone called his attention, and he looked away from the little nightmare to receive the compliments of some gentlemen with whom he was vaguely acquainted in London.

When Devlin looked for the redhead again, she was just approaching the quieter young lady she had been with in the tea rooms. She grasped her friend's hands and swung her hands in excitement, causing several glances her way, not all amused. Devlin grinned. She had no notion, he was sure, of the eyes upon her, whether amused or not. Her friend attempted to quiet her, much more aware of the attention drawn, but she jumped again, this time backing into a gentleman, who immediately asked her to dance.

Devlin watched as that gentleman, in a decent coat and well-arranged cravat, made insinuating eyes at her in the set, thinking, as Devlin briefly had in the tea house, that the young redhead had sought out his attention, by *conveniently* bumping him. Having watched her disastrous progress this evening, Devlin knew this was untrue and wondered how she would receive the gentleman's attentions, and she seemed as open and enthusiastic as before — but not more so. Her dance partner seemed annoyed, and her expression was then puzzled. It seemed he was rude, for she flushed as only a redhead can, and looked to her feet. However, this caused disaster, and she tripped over her slippers at the next step, careered into another couple, and ended by pushing her partner from his feet in an impotent bid to get control, falling herself in the process.

Devlin guffawed, and several others looked at him, only to join in. Soon laughter, much of it mocking, surrounded the collapsed couple, and the orchestra halted. The gentleman got up, the girl's mama (or perhaps chaperone) rushed to her and she, blushing, joined in the mocking laughter with good grace. Her partner vanished. The music started again, and Devlin saw the mother deposit her daughter on a bench by the wall, obviously annoyed.

He was surprised at himself that he had given way to laughter, but that girl was just *so* ...! She was ridiculous, but he was aware that she had been held up to ridicule further, because of him. He had met and mingled with the most elite of this town, he had been flattered by many. His rank had encouraged the open laughter; this small world had taken a lead from him, and he was sorry for it.

As he passed the bench of abandoned women, he suddenly stopped at her and asked her to dance, to alleviate his guilt somewhat.

She looked up at him, smiling, only a little shyly. 'We have not been introduced but I know you are Viscount Devlin, are you not? Well, I am Eloise Travers, and I am pleased to meet you.'

She held out a forthright hand and he was not even surprised any more. He bowed over it, rather than shaking it, however, and a young lady beside her gasped in awe.

He led her to the dance, and she skipped beside him to match his long stride. He could not imagine why he was walking this fast, just that there was something that must be done. The orchestra struck up a waltz, and he said, with some regret, 'I should take you back! I should be presented by the master of ceremonies, presuming this to be your first waltz.'

'How did you guess? It is my first ever assembly here, although I am twenty-two you know.'

'You look about eighteen.'

'Oh, here comes Mama, *will* you dance with me sir? She is a trifle annoyed at me right now. I can later say to the master of ceremonies that I waltzed in Halifax previously.'

'*Are* there Assembly rooms in Halifax?'

'Yes, I assure you.'

He looked into her merry eyes and the freckles that would make a map of Northumberland if joined up and sighed. 'If you promise not to crush my toes, I will risk social reproval and dance with you.'

'Oh...!' she was going to be deadly honest again, but he moved her along to the dance floor.

'It was *my* laughter that began your embarrassment, Miss Travers,' Devlin confessed. 'I apologise.'

She blushed but looked back at him smiling shyly. 'It is quite alright. The only *good* thing about my clumsiness is that it provides amusement to my friends!' He saw that though she was resigned, she was somewhat embarrassed, too.

'Not only to your friends and not all the amusement is without judgment.'

'I only care about my friends' amusement, why should I care for others?'

He wondered at the origins of this confidence and was stunned to conclude that she meant it.

He turned her under his arm in the figures of the waltz and she tripped and had to be steadied by his free hand.

'Look at Miss Ottley,' she gushed, her eyes turning in that lady's direction, 'how very gracefully she achieves it.'

'Yes.'

'I could *never* have that grace.'

'I suppose not,' he agreed, looking across at Miss Ottley's pointed toe.

'You were there to see her at the tea rooms, my lord, were you not?' she said, looking at him confidingly. As his lips pursed, she added airily, 'You need not say so. You are the *new* viscount — I expect the duke must wish you to marry soon.'

'He does,' he agreed laconically to her excessive frankness.

'Our Miss Ottley would make a *splendid* duchess one day.'

'I suppose she would.'

'She is beautiful, and accomplished and kind...'

'She was not kind to *you*,' said Devlin with an ironically raised brow, 'she laughed when you fell.'

'Well, so did *you*...!' She had blushed but looked at him naughtily to hide her discomfort.

'You *make* me laugh. I have not laughed in a year, and yet on the occasions I have seen you, I have laughed three times.'

'I am embarrassed, but glad.'

'And, confidentially, Miss Ottley's governess does *not* like her,'

'Pardon?' Her eyes were like saucers as she looked her question.

'This is between us. I should not mention it, except that you might continue to be Miss Ottley's champion to a more naïve gentleman.' He was divulging his small investigation that he had made only to perhaps hear words from the beneficiary of cake, that might lift him from his state of ennui and encourage him to make this life changing decision with some small enthusiasm, perhaps. 'I visited the governess in her poor rooms. She was cast off by the Ottley family with little support. Miss Ottley meets her to be *seen* to be compassionate, I presume.'

'No!'

'I believe so. The poor lady attends for the tea and crumpets she can have but once a week.'

'She *starves?*' said Miss Travers, looking distressed. 'Pray, what is her direction?'

He reassured her concern. 'She will not starve for the foreseeable future. I saw to it. Neither will she visit the tea house, at least not at Miss Ottley's insistence.'

'Oh.'

'You sound disappointed.'

'I am. I thought you would make a lovely husband for the finest lady in our town.' Her large green eyes sought his again, looking for understanding, 'Because you were so kind, not because you were the son of a duke, which I did not know at all,' she excused herself. 'Only that you were not vulgar like the gentleman in the striped waistcoat, Mr Prince, and that you were handsome.'

'It is *good* you find me handsome,' he said, a trifle smugly. It was a tease, and she heard it as such.

'You should not dissemble,' she laughed at him in the friendliest manner. 'You *know* you are handsome.'

Devlin took her astounding frankness stoically. 'Yes. I came here at my father's bidding to find a wife. Miss Ottley was proposed as such, and she does indeed fit the list of attributes my papa gave me, but …!' She was enthralled by his candour and listening attentively. His natural reserve cracked easily under her open gaze. 'My brother died of influenza. He is the true viscount and heir, and his betrothed ought to have been his duchess. But now it is only I, a man who has no ambition at all, and less ability, who can fill this post. Miss Ottley might have helped me, but I do not wish for an unkind wife. Instead, I think I have found the wife who will make me laugh. I have not laughed in an age!'

She blinked, far from understanding. He tried again.

'I would like permission to approach your father, Miss Travers.'

'*Excuse me?...* It cannot be. You are too fine to ...! What on earth can you like about *me*?'

'I like that there is one spiral of hair that is sticking straight up tonight,' he began. She tried to dance and flatten her curl at once and stumbled again. 'I think I might like to look at *that* over breakfast, rather than Miss Ottley's perfect profile.'

'No! *Nobody* would prefer that...!'

'You have a much more interesting face than your heroine, you know,' he said, near her ear. She trembled, and it made him happy to affect her. 'I have seen a hundred expressions on that face tonight. Concern, excitement, compassion, enthusiasm, naughtiness, friendliness, joy. I could list more.' He said, 'I think *you* have looked at *me* a deal, too,' he saw that she blushed consciously, and he laughed. 'What did *you* see?'

He saw, in her open face, the hesitation, then the decision to be candid. 'Oh ...' she mused, 'haughtiness, reserve, kindness, superiority, *ennui*, patience, and a little sadness and despair, I believe. I saw it when you danced with Miss Ottley. I thought it a strange sight for a gentleman dancing with such a beauty.'

'It is because I was imagining breakfast looking at her face. I am now imagining *your* face over breakfast, what do you see in my expression now?'

She gazed back directly, unaware that more and more people were paying attention at their demeanour: the obvious intensity of their conversation. 'Wickedness, teasing ... perhaps amusement,' she answered.

'Do you like me, Miss Travers?'

She looked down, shaken. 'You are extremely wicked to ask this in the middle of a waltz. We have never conversed…!'

'It seems I have conversed with you all evening. Your eyes told me tales, even across the ballroom.'

'This kind of thing does not *happen*. It is absurd!' But her eyes looked at him for reassurance. Then she shook her head as though to clear it. 'But … what do you know of my family?'

'Nothing, except that your mother and father conduct themselves as gentlefolk this evening.' He held her eyes. 'Tell me of them.'

She looked at him askance, but after a moment did as she was bid. 'My father is a baronet, and a gentleman indeed. But unfortunately for your impulsive plan, I should tell you that my mother's family is in trade, and Papa increased his own wealth because of it. *Your* father would not find the match acceptable; I am sure.' She seemed a little sad at this, to Devlin's delight. She looked up, 'It must just be a whim of yours, since you are still sad at your brother's passing and feel crushed by your duty. I might make you laugh, but you could do so much better.' She leaned forward a little earnestly, making others stare. 'I am dreadfully clumsy, you know, and though I try, I possess *no* dignity *whatsoever*.'

'I know. Somehow, I like it.'

'You are foolish, then,' she admonished him, in a way he found enchanting. 'Even *I* do not like it, and your father will *certainly* not.'

Devlin played a trick on her and stroked her palm with one finger as they danced. She trembled and blushed. He was affecting her, but himself too. As when she had gestured earlier, it rebounded on him, and he held his breath. But she became rather serious in her gaze, rebuking him silently.

'Leave that to me.,' he reassured her. 'Are you ***willing***?'

'You are much too handsome for me,' she protested. 'You must think of what is due to *yourself*.'

'You are too adorable for *me*. You think only of others.'

She blushed. 'Is *this* how London gentlemen behave to unmarried ladies?'

'You will *never* know,' he said, grasping the hand he held a little tighter, 'for I will have you as my betrothed before any other can steal you next Season.'

At this she giggled, her tension lightened by his absurdity.

'Good!' he nodded, as she smiled back warmly, 'I can make *you* laugh, too! A better grounding for marriage than any other, don't you feel?' He had trapped her in the steps of this waltz and then thrown a great deal on her, but really, there had been a man who had danced with her earlier who had given Devlin pause by his attentive manner towards the oblivious Miss Travers. The redhead was too precious to escape him. To calm her nerves, he asked, 'What other qualities *do* you seek in a husband?'

She looked down in contemplation, and as she raised her eyes, they were hazy. 'Someone kind.' She looked off, as though something occurred to her. 'But I know that *you* are that, ever since the tea rooms.' He smiled as she looked off again seriously thinking. Her gravity was adorable to him 'Someone who will not mind my clumsy mistakes.' Then she looked up at him, eyes wide in surprise. 'Oh, *that* is you, *too*!'

Her face was a little chubby, her nose a trifle snub. Her eyes were a lovely green, and he tried to infuse his own with warmth as she danced away from him for the moment. He did not like the worry that he saw there. She met his eyes for a long moment as they held arms aloft and danced side by side in a slow circle. What she saw in his made her smile a dimpled, delightful smile.

'Will you give me permission?' he reiterated.

'Oh. Very well then.' She tripped with nervousness as she said so, and Devlin, shockingly, put an arm around her waist. A few gasps surrounded them.

Her papa was frowning as the viscount approached to return her.

'I wish to speak to you, sir, at your earliest opportunity,' Devlin said, bowing. There were more than a few eyes on the encounter and the grizzly baronet sniffed.

'You are Viscount Devlin, are you not?' said the father, gruffly.

'Yes, sir.'

'Hm! I know your father.'

'Perhaps then, our conversation might go more smoothly.'

***

The viscount informed his father on his return to London.

The duke looked up from his port. 'You became betrothed to a Miss Travers of no particular fortune?'

'You know her father, Papa. Sir Peter Travers.'

'Good man ... but how does that count? Is his daughter so beautiful?'

The viscount smiled in deprecation. 'She is loud and clumsy and enthusiastic and *adorable*.'

'*Not* a suitable duchess, then,' sniffed his father, eying him narrowly.

'But there is *one* advantage, Papa. If I marry Miss Travers I will laugh a great deal,' his father frowned, but he was intrigued, and Devlin knew it. 'There will be joy in this house again. You will like her, Papa, for it is impossible not to.'

His father raised his brows.

Devlin leaned forward, confidentially. 'And I think I can guarantee you many, many ducal heirs, Your Grace.'

'Like *that*, is it?' the duke replied. 'I'll invite them to Radcliffe.'

***

Despite Eloise knocking over an epergne in the afternoon room, two old friends met and agreed to the betrothal, the duke a little reluctantly, with more of a resigned, rather than enthusiastic, air.

But over dinner, his future daughter-in-law suddenly informed him seriously, 'Now that I have met Your Grace, I suddenly prefer *not* to be a duchess for a long, long time.'

The duke, whose misery had been better disguised than his son's at the loss of his first heir and beloved boy, but who had also smiled less since that tragedy, dropped his fork. As Eloise's mother berated her quietly, the duke let out a huge guffaw that shook the rafters. His son caught it and joined in, and the embarrassed Travers parents eventually gave into it too — and all eating was suspended for ten minutes, the duke waving his napkin around every time he tried to stop laughing.

It was the end of awkward formality, and of the tension Eloise's parents had felt in case she might do something worse than knock over a family heirloom. Four weeping individuals caught each other's eyes in turn and re-experienced the ridiculousness of Eloise's reassurance to Devlin's papa.

'You are all laughing at me,' said Eloise in a chiding tone, 'but I shall not mind it!'

This merely increased the hilarity.

'Let us have the wedding sooner,' said the duke, eventually, mopping his tears, 'It'll do the old place good to have the little one live here.'

As the party left the dining hall, Devlin held Eloise back and pulled her into a little chamber adjacent.

'Viscount!' She protested. He cupped her red curls with his hand, and she said, 'Is my hair on end again? It is independent of the comb on occasion, I am afraid.'

'It is lovely, and you are lovely, and now...,' he was nearer and nearer her and her legs were giving way — therefore, as a gentleman should, he held her up, his arm about her waist bringing her close to him. He bent and kissed her lips and she held on to him.

'Mama...' she said, as she turned, furiously blushing, to go.

'She will not look for you for a while.' He put his hand around her waist again, this time from the back, pulling her close to his chest. 'The rules for betrothed couples are a little laxer than for an unmarried lady,' he said into her ear.

'Let me go, my lord, for I fear my face is about to display a horrid purple hue. I am *so* embarrassed.'

'How shall we overcome this problem?' The voice in her ear was low and smooth and was causing her to catch her breath. 'I do not wish for a purple-hued wife,' he continued, making her giggle, 'but I find I must kiss you very, very often.'

She turned in his arms and put her face to his chest, hiding there. 'Perhaps then, we should practice a little more so that I become accustomed?'

'An excellent notion!' he approved, stroking her curls, 'But did you like the *first* kiss, my purple princess?'

'Oh, very much!' she enthused, in the way he adored. 'I am not sorry *at all* now that Miss Ottley missed her chance. Even though she is my idol, I think I might *slap* her if she came to take you away.'

'You would do right, my darling,' he said dotingly, caressing her.

'I am so *very* happy, Devlin. Let us practice more!' she said, standing on her tiptoes to accommodate him.

Oscar Devlin did as he was told, his kisses lingering on her upturned face. He pulled away. 'We must find your mama and the tea now,' he told her lovingly, 'the rules of betrothal are not so *very* different, after all.'

'I expected so. You, my viscount, are simply wicked.'

'And you, my redhead, are simply delightful.' As she gazed around and up at the enormously high ceilings of the corridor, the viscount added, 'Do you think you will like living here?'

'Oh, yes. It is just like home you know!' she giggled, 'except that one could hold a carriage race in your salon.'

'Mmm,' he said, making a sound as her elbow nearly dislodged a decorative plate on a stand in a console table. 'I must remember to have the breakables removed to a height above your arms.'

His redhead sighed, sadly, 'You underestimate the peculiar talents of your betrothed if you think that will be sufficient.'

'I cannot wait to see what havoc you will wreck, my love.' But he grinned as he said so and Eloise held his arm, smiling at the interested servants as she passed.

Chapter Nine

Eva and the Stolen Kisses

Sir Rupert Danes stood opposite the woman he had just married a scant half hour ago, looking down on her from his full height. She was a foot shorter than his six foot figure and stood with her head bent, eyes lowered and hands clasped in front of her.

'I called you to my study, a room you shall not enter again, because I wanted a private place to speak to you. No one enters here but a maid once a week and Bishop, my butler. This is a rule that will include you, my lady.'

She peeped up at him from beneath her lids and nodded appeasingly. He frowned back terribly, and she lowered her eyes once more.

'This match is one made by our families, and as such I respect it, but you must understand your limits, Lady Danes.'

She looked up again, astonished, and her hand pointed to her chest as though to mime *'Me?'* Then she smiled a brief smile and sought his eye. *'I am Lady Danes,'* the look said, *'isn't that funny?'*

He frowned more dreadfully then, and she cowered somewhat and lowered her eyes.

'I told you before the betrothal that you will live in my home, but that certain ... responsibilities of a wife ... will not fall upon you.'

She frowned at this, as though puzzled, but did not look up.

She was, he reflected, very young, and seemed not to understand. Her puzzlement made him flush a little, though he held himself taller.

'I wish to have as little to do with you possible.' He coughed, realising how impolite this was, but hardened. All must be said today.

She looked at the carpet and one small foot seemed to be following a scroll on the pattern with a pointed toe.

'You understand me?' He said, flushed again, 'I do not wish for children.'

She clasped her hands behind her then, and looked to the side, to the bookcases.

'You will be informed if I should wish you to accompany me to a social engagement, where you will merely be on my arm, and not speak.'

Her head was moving, looking around the room, but avoiding his gaze. She seemed to be thinking of something else. Merely gazing vacuously around.

'Are you listening to me?' he said, hardly able to believe her inattention.

The head swivelled to the down position again and she nodded vigorously, looking startled. The hands began to wring.

He lifted his head again. 'I have no more to tell you. I will send instructions through the servants. Good day, my lady.'

It was a dismissal. She looked up at last, her big brown eyes contrasted with her lighter curls, and she sighed as though a schoolgirl who had just finished being lectured by her mistress. She smiled up at him and one leg retreated without his volition. He reclaimed his dignity quickly. 'You may go!' he said coldly, since she had not taken the earlier hint.

'Oh yes!' she said. Suddenly, she took his hand in one of hers, stood on her tiptoes and kissed his cheek. 'Goodnight my lord,' she said, smiling, and tripped from the room. Danes staggered back until he felt the desk behind him and sat on the edge.

What was that?

***

Danes heard her before he saw her next morning. She was singing a country air, a happy little ditty, as she tripped down the stairs. He judged by the change in tone that she had entered the dining room for breakfast, but then she must have left it quickly, for he heard the song again, coming towards him. He trembled. In rage, he thought, or at least in consternation.

Sure enough, his study door opened and a head of light curls appeared, threaded with pink ribbon. A distinct smell of attar of roses hung in the air.

'Did you not hear my instructions, Lady Danes? He said foully.

'Oh, but see,' she said pointing down, 'I have not put a foot inside. Only, breakfast is ready, and I thought you might join me.'

It did not seem dignified to say that her foot may not be in, but her head certainly was, so he only said, 'I will not. And do not open that door ever again.'

Her face had fallen briefly, but she closed the door and went off humming the air.

He did not hear or see her again that day, to his intense relief, but that evening he wondered enough to say to Bishop when he came in with a warm wine, 'What did her ladyship do today?'

'As to that I am not at all sure, my lord. She went out after breakfast and came back in the afternoon and retired to her chamber. I could enquire of her maid.'

'Yes, yes there is no need to give me an itinerary.'

'Yes, my lord, but you might wish to know that Lady Danes has for the last hour been sitting on a chair in the hall.'

'What? Why?'

'I do not know, my lord, her ladyship did not inform me. I offered her some refreshments, but she refused and only let me send for a shawl for her fifteen minutes ago. It is chilly in the hall, my lord.'

'No doubt.' Danes said coldly. Then he sighed and said in a bored tone, 'She may do as she wishes, I suppose.'

When Bishop came back to take the tray, Danes looked up from his book to say 'Still?'

'Yes, my lord.'

He let the butler leave and went back to his book, but he found that he could not concentrate, and he moved into the hall, as though to bed. He saw her from the corner of his eye as she called to him and he stopped, looking over his shoulder at her.

'My lord at last!' she said, and ran to him before he could avoid it, grasping an arm and using it for purchase as she stood on her toes and kissed his cheek. There was a miasma of chill about her, but her lips seemed warm. 'Goodnight, my lord,' she said, as though she was escaping something with relief, and went ahead of him, fairly dancing up the stairs.

He grunted at the attack, for so he felt it to be, but she was already gone before he could catch his wits, and he saw a footman with a less than blank look on his face trying not to appear interested. Danes backed into the study.

He would call her to him after breakfast. What was she doing? He had made himself plain as to the borders of their relationship, or transaction as he called it to himself. Did she have romantic notions, or a seductive soul? She was foolish in either case. The line had to be drawn.

***

'I did not think I should see this room again,' she remarked after he had had her summoned after breakfast.

'You are impudent!'

She adopted the pose of yesterday again, a schoolgirl about to be lectured to.

'I wish to speak with you where we are sure not to be interrupted.'

Bishop came in with some tea. The minx giggled.

'Behave!' he said, sounding like a school master indeed. Bishop left silently.

'I beg your pardon, My Lord. But it was so amusing after you had just said...!'

'Quiet!'

She obeyed immediately, gazing at her toes. If only she were a little older, she might be dignified enough to accept her fate, and proud enough not to annoy him so. He could not shake himself of the notion that she was still suppressing giggles. 'You shall not see this room again,' she peeped up at him, looking a little dubious. He ignored the expression. 'I called you here to ask what you have been about. Your *behaviour...*,' he emphasised the word with grim intent, '... of the previous two evenings must not continue.'

She looked up and blinked. 'I am afraid I must disobey you!' she said, her throat constrained. She looked fearful, cowered at his furious shock, and looked down again, taking a step back as she did so.

'I beg your pardon?'

'....disobey...,' was the only thing he caught in her mumbling reply. She turned her head as though he might strike her and cowered further.

He pulled himself up. 'You shall *not* disobey me!'

She put up her hands shaking them in a refuting gesture, and braved another look at him, saying in an apologetic tone, 'Oh, I shall not disobey you in *any* other thing, I assure you, my lord. But in *this*...!'

'What do you hope to achieve by this ridiculous behaviour?'

'Oh, *nothing at all!* You do not think I *wished* to freeze myself waiting for you in the hall, did you?'

He looked down at her, keeping calm with difficulty.

'It is just that I *must*,' she continued, a plea in her large brown eyes.

'You intend to *continue*? When I have *expressly forbidden* it?' he said, unable to conceive of it.

'So sorry!' she said in a small voice.

He retreated behind his desk and sat, trilling his fingertips on the surface in an effort to reduce his anger. She was clearly terrified. Why was she so obstinate about this one thing? But if one gave certain people an inch, they would take a mile. 'I am on my guard now. I shall not permit it.'

'Oh, that would be *worse*, for I should just have to make attempt after attempt and lengthen the whole...! Oh, *please* do not.'

Finally, he asked the question he did not wish to. He did indeed, wish to ask her no questions at all, for questions suggested an interest he was far from feeling. But the shock of the last two nights must end. It had disturbed him horribly. He had spent two hours last night considering her motives and reliving the dreadful events in his head. He could not continue thus. And so, he asked, 'But *why?*'

'I swore an oath to my grandfather as he was dying.'

When she did not continue, he must. A death bed oath, for the lord's sake. 'What oath?'

'That whoever I married I should only make grandpapa *one* promise, that I should kiss him good night every night, as he did grandmama. He said it cured all ills.'

'And you agreed.'

'Of course.'

'Lady Danes.' He said, with an assumption of calm. 'No doubt your grandfather's marriage was built on affection. But it is not so for us, and I have made it clear that you must not hope for more.'

'Oh, I do *not!*' she reassured him, in a manner that suggested relief rather than sadness.

While this reassured him, it pricked at his pride somewhat. However, he acknowledged her agreement by saying reasonably, 'Then you must see, in common sense, that in *this* marriage the oath does not apply.'

'It applies because I made it. And of course, *when* I made it, I could not guess that it would be *you* who...' He felt a prick of annoyance at her evident regret. She looked up at him with the enormous brown eyes again and said plaintively, 'I wish to obey you in everything, my lord, but I must keep my previous promise to grandpapa.' Tears spilled over, 'You cannot wish me to disobey *my grandfather's last wish?*'

Females! He thought, exasperated, looking in horror at the wet cheeks. 'I tell you; *it is not applicable in this case!*' he said furiously.

She cowered and trembled anew at his tone.

'Good. So, we are agreed then?' he had never thought that he would seek anyone's agreement before now. 'You will desist.'

She gave a little craven mew and he said, 'Go!'

That night, as he crossed the hall, a little bullet rushed at him, struggled to reach up, and kissed his cheek, running off. 'Goodnight,' she breathed after the kiss, but so quickly he barely heard her.

'You...!' he called after her. She ran up the stairs, almost bent double into the cower and away from him.

***

He had married her with no desire to be either kind or cruel. It was simply a way to fulfil his duty to his grandfather. Their respective grandfathers had been friends. She was the daughter of a marquis of an old house, almost as old as his baronetcy. It might be said that in marrying him she was degrading her rank (if one cared about the rank of mere females), but of course his baronetcy was richer than many a marquis's house. Females had no rank at all except through marriage. Their father's rank was as nothing to them, except that a duke's daughter might sit higher at a dinner table than an earl's wife. The respect a man of rank's daughter received was due only to her proximity to male status.

He, on the other hand, might have chosen a bride where he will, and indeed Lady Georgina, the daughter of the Duke of Solis had looked towards him, and her father mentioned it to him casually in the club. This kind of thing happened frequently, but he had no real wish to marry. The succession was secure since his brother had produced brats too numerous to mention, so he had no need to. But there was the mention of an old marriage arrangement (written when the girl was but three months old, and he was eight) in grandpapa's will. Then there had been the death of his father which had given him the barony. He did not much miss his father, who had been both cold and occasionally harsh, and in the years of his adulthood they had not much met.

The marriage arrangement had been at the back of the baronet's head, a last wish from a grandpapa who had been kind to him when he was a child. Such things did not always come to fruition in any case, so he had felt no guilt at not pursuing the case. But then there was the incident of the duke's remarks over cards and another coincidence: earlier that same day he had seen Lady Eva Laurence with her stepmama in a draper's shop, and he heard and saw a good deal about how the girl was treated.

'Now dear...!' would say the father to the stepmama when she was monumentally rude to his only offspring, pulling her up for thirty lapses of behaviour in a minute, lapses that seemed to the baronet to be spurious, and the harridan turned on her husband at even this light reproof.

'If I, who stand as a mother to the girl, may not correct her bearing, who *may*?'

The girl stood with a vague look on her face, that rather mirrored the father's, Danes had thought, and the woman continued, 'She is in a daze again! She does not heed a *thing* I say...!'

The girl had looked around, confused, 'You said I should straighten up stepmama, and I have. I always listen to what you say.'

'She calls me stepmama still! Do you hear her, Henry? Everyone notes that she has no affection for me whatsoever.'

'My dear Eva, you must call the marchioness Mama you know!'

'I wish to oblige you, Papa, but it does not come readily to my tongue, since it makes me cry to say the word, and miss my own Mama anew.'

The marquis looked as though he missed her mother, too, but saw his second wife glare.

'Well, you must try, my love!'

'Yes Papa.'

'She always says *yes*, and nothing changes at all.'

The girl looked crestfallen, and Danes knew the merest touch of sympathy. The stepmama was quite dreadful.

He moved off, reflecting that this young thing was his partner by arrangement, but had no idea of doing a thing about it until that evening at the club when the duke spoke of his daughter, and he suddenly saw the benefit of not being bothered with this sort of thing again. 'You are probably unaware, Your Grace, that there exists a family marriage arrangement already.'

'I see!' said the duke. He sighed. 'Now I must tell my Georgina. She will have hysterics, no doubt. It will be time for me to go to the Cheltenham Race meet.'

Danes was surprised at this violence of feeling from the duke's daughter, since he had only met Lady Georgina on two occasions, neither notable. It seemed he had escaped a wilfulness of temper that contrasted with the girl in the drapers.

Or so he had thought.

He determined at that moment, that an arranged marriage might be beneficial to himself and Miss Laurence, both.

***

That afternoon, considering his wife's continued defiance, Danes forbore to go home for dinner, and instead stayed in the club late. Later than his cronies, who made up the more temperate members. He even drank a deal of wine, but he gave a smile to Bennet, a man he had gone to school with, and said, upon his inquiry, 'I've outrun her tonight!'

Bennet, married himself, merely smiled at this drunken remark, and drank on.

It was two o'clock in the morning when the baronet arrived home. He entered by the mews' door and put a finger to his mouth when he came to the hall, hushing Bishop, before the butler could speak.

He divested himself of outerwear, followed the footman with the candelabra upstairs, feeling pleasantly victorious. He had reached his room by an unsound path when he saw the half-asleep figure on a chair opposite his room. She pounced, kissed, smiled and was gone, with a soft, 'Goodnight, my lord.'

***

The von Bergen party could not be avoided. Danes sent a message to his lady that she would accompany him to an ambassadorial dinner this evening and she should dress accordingly. She was in a velvet cloak, a gauze shawl over her light brown curls, when he came to collect her in the hall.

They entered the carriage together. 'Do not talk this evening.' He told her once inside.

She looked at him vaguely, then seemed to concentrate. He remembered that she seemed to have a literal understanding and added, 'That is, you may talk, but only briefly, in answer to remarks that may be made to you.' He looked over at her. 'I trust you understand how to conduct yourself in company.'

'I think I do,' she said in her vague voice.

Never mind, he thought, her presence would relieve him of the attention of three ladies, one married, who were to be there tonight. His looking glass might suggest one reason he was pursued, i.e. rich brown locks, and a Germanic face, which was often called handsome — but he suspected the gold deposited in his bank was more significant. Whatever it was, it was tiresome. Tonight, the marriage he had come to rue (after the nightly attacks) might finally prove useful.

'Mr von Bergen,' he said smoothly, 'I must present to you, my wife.'

'Wife? Danes?' came some chatter behind him, 'And *what* is she wearing?'

Danes' smile stayed in place, but he looked down at his wife, whom he had not much regarded after she took off her cloak and scarf, and saw the gown. It was round gown in brown silk, made over from one that had obviously adorned a larger lady.

Brown? A round gown at least ten years out of date? There was nothing else to do than hold his head higher and smile at the dignitaries and their wives and daughters.

True to his instructions, his Lady Danes did not comment first, but answered all questions in a docile fashion. Throughout dinner, many looks were sent his way and hers, but she ate with apparent relish, smiled when called on to talk, and looked around the room with the vague gaze that seemed to be her habit.

A late visitor was announced. Prince Werther Starhemberg. The prince, a personable young man a few years Danes' junior, apologised to the Von Bergers, blaming an unexpected pothole.

Dane's wife, who had paid little attention to the entrance, perhaps not listening to the announcement, now looked up at the voice. She stood up from the table, her first dereliction of good manners.

'My Prince!' she cried to the astonishment of all.

'*Eva!* You here?' Prince Werther's delighted voice rang out, 'I heard you got married, little one, and was honour bound to visit you tomorrow.' He had come towards her and grasped her shoulders. Danes froze.

The prince turned to the open-mouthed diners. 'Oh, you must pardon us! The last time I saw my little sister here she saved my life you know.' He put a hand to her curls, but she ducked and, quite shockingly for Dane's notion of his new wife, slapped his highness on the wrist.

'Do not ruffle my hair,' she ordered, 'it has been done for the occasion!'

'You look very grown up!' said the prince, laughing down at her. He held her off a little, making a face, 'But what a dreadful gown!'

'Isn't it?' Dane's wife agreed. 'It is grandmama's you know.'

The prince had voiced it for all the company. Everyone looked to Danes. He ignored the gazes and instead stood and held out his hand to the prince. 'I must introduce myself, your highness, I am Sir Rupert Danes, husband of your, ah, little sister.'

The prince shook his hand with enthusiasm, and Danes felt the temperature in the room lower.

'Oh, pleased to meet you. Sorry for interrupting, but it *is* good to see my little sister again,' the man said, turning to Danes with his open good-natured face.

'You are related?' Danes enquired politely.

'Oh, somewhere or other,' the prince said vaguely, 'but we were brought up together, you know.' He turned to Eva again. 'But why are you wearing grandmama Sutton's dress?'

'I have no evening gowns, you see,' his wife answered blandly.

'My wife,' said Danes to the assembled company, 'is newly married, and has not yet had time to buy her trousseau.'

'Did the wicked stepmother send you off without a groat?' asked the prince.

She nodded and looked a little mischievous. This last had been said in a lowered voice, only Danes and his lady able to hear it.

'Never mind, Gretchen and Mama are here and will take you shopping tomorrow.'

'Will they? Oh, how lovely!'

The prince turned back to the diners, 'I beg your pardon. Our meeting has delayed you all.' With a last squeeze of her shoulders, he left to sit at the other side of the table at his appointed seat next to the ambassador.

On the carriage ride home Danes was desperate not to ask questions. He did not want the connection, but he supposed that he should not have been *quite* so disinterested as he was, since it might lead to the sort of problems he had experienced tonight.

'Why did you not buy yourself a suitable gown today?' he asked testily, 'I told you we were to attend a diplomatic party.'

'I had no money.'

'You know that I will give you pin money.'

'But you have not.'

'I did not see it as urgent.'

'It is not urgent really, my cousin Sarah paid for our nuncheon the other day, *and* bought me some gloves, too.'

'It is a pity she did not buy you an evening gown.'

'Oh no, how could I ask it of her? Her husband is only a curate, you know.'

'You could not pay for your own lunch?'

'I told you; I had no money.'

'Surely you had something of your spinster's allowance.'

'I had no allowance.'

'You must have had ...! What age are you?'

'Twenty.'

'No allowance? What about during your Seasons.'

'I did not attend parties, you know. I did not have a Season. Abigail had a Season, and I was just there.'

'Who is Abigail?'

'My stepmother's daughter.'

'This is ridiculous. Did not your Papa provide you with funds?'

'He used to before Mama died, gift me pennies when he remembered. But now ...!'

He was silent and the carriage bowled on through the London Streets until they neared their home.

Just as he was about to alight, she, who had him in close quarters, did not shirk her advantage, she leant over the footwell and kissed his cheek just as he had opened the door, saying, 'Goodnight, my lord.'

***

What was to be done with Lady Danes? It was, perhaps, a wrong decision on his part to marry at all. He had entered into this alliance with the approval of her father, of course. The man had seemed grateful — not quite to be rid of her, but for her to remove from his house, '... *for the new marchioness and she do not go on well,*' the marquis had said somewhat sadly. The avaricious marchioness had tried to discuss settlements with Danes, but he had scorned to discuss such with her and given her a very cold response, requesting an interview with her lord alone. There had been, in the eye of the repressed young Lady Eva, a gleam of something at his behaviour. She evidently approved.

After the settlement conversation with the marquis, he had requested that before a betrothal was formalised, he would also like to speak to the young lady. The marquis' demeanour, he now knew, was like his daughter's. He had appeared, for at least some of the time, to wander in his thoughts, agreeing blandly when recalled. Danes had never known a high-ranking aristocrat with such an uncommanding presence. The man seemed to have an animal awareness of sounds in the hall, however, and looked alert and afraid both, briefly. It could be fairly said that he was a man who lived under the cat's paw.

The marquis agreed to the interview with his daughter, 'For,' Danes had said, 'I will take no unwilling bride.'

The marchioness was not happy to be asked to leave the room by her lord, 'So that the young people may discuss the arrangements.' He explained to her.

'Oh, but I am afraid the *proprieties* forbid it!' tittered the marchioness.

Danes, whose repulsion of this woman was becoming a taste in his mouth, said, with a cold eye, 'If you think so my lady, I shall bow to your wish and not come again to this house.'

She recoiled, then uttered playfully, 'Oh, you are such an ardent suitor, Sir Rupert. Very well, I can allow it, but will leave the door ajar to protect the proprieties, you know.'

And, thought Danes, to listen to the conversation. He had no intention of allowing it. The girl must be at least free to reject him. It was possible she had another connection, a gentleman she preferred. He had looked at Lady Eva sitting, eyes downcast, meekly awaiting him. She seemed to be wearing a very dull dress indeed.

He gestured her to the farthest window, and she followed him, where he told her in a low voice what he proposed and why (the grandfather's arrangement) and that he wanted a wife in name only. If she had a previous attachment, or if she hoped for more companionship in marriage — this he could not provide, but that he would leave her reasonably unfettered if she did not sully his name with scandal. As with the marquis, she seemed not to hear much of his peroration, but she did say that she had no attachment, and she would be honoured to accept his offer. 'For I do not suppose' she had added almost to herself, 'that I shall receive another.'

He left the house after signing the settlements, but he had been rather flattened by the whole affair. He had imagined that she might greet his offer with more ... gratitude, for he was rescuing her from the dreadful marchioness, after all. Her answer had been meek, but her manner a little vague.

But she was not a designing female, he was sure. She did not have the wit. She was presentable, would be more so when suitably dressed (how did the marchioness justify having a young girl so ill-prepared for respectable company?) and she was biddable.

Danes, on account of the actions of one designing female ten years ago, had no desire at all to dangle with females. His heart had been soft then, and deeply wounded when the woman who said so many loving words to him had married a man of higher rank. Now his heart was a steel cage, only one or two close friends ever allowed to visit, and he had nothing at all to do with females, beyond relatives or wives of friends.

His life was full and sufficient. He was firm but fair to his servants and dependants, he crushed his enemies without mercy, and was known as rigid, stone-faced and someone not to cross. He seemed to be of a rather joyless disposition, but all his family were — with the exception of the roguish grandfather he had loved. His friends were from the more respectable class of gentlemen-about-town, not given to the excesses of whoring or gambling. He drove and rode excellently, he advised his own man of business on the stock market, for he often met with the merchant class in coffee houses and understood them. He had an appreciation of the arts, but this was cultivated rather than innate — but he enjoyed the opera a great deal.

Now, though, he was married — a condition that he had thought would be to his advantage (and somewhat to hers) and would not otherwise disturb his life. But now he saw how naive he was to have thought that there was no possibility of disturbing him. His wife's dress had shamed him the other night, and indeed what he remembered of her other clothes did so to — he had neglected to give her pin money on arrival and had not informed her that her visits to linen drapers and dress makers and milliners could be simply resolved by sending the bills to their home. A marquis' daughter had come to him without a penny in her purse, or a good dress on her back. It was intolerable.

But clearly, he had forbidden her approach him and he had not paid attention enough to her needs. He had thought that, given her position in life before marriage, she would slot into the household and order things as she wished, but this was obviously not within the rights he had described to her, nor the rights that she had known to assert. Taking on a cowed, obedient female meant that he had to establish her prestige in the household *himself.* The other thing, that awful thing before bed, weighed on him, but clearly, he must deal with her rights first. He had no desire to talk to her about this (or indeed anything else) so when the commotion in the hall had announced the arrival of the prince along with some ladies, he had the butler summon in his highness to his study.

'Forgive me for not welcoming you in the hall, Prince Werther,' Danes began, standing from his desk and going around to shake hands with the prince.

'Danes! Not at all. We are just awaiting Eva put on her bonnet and we shall be gone in a trice anyway.'

'I called you aside to give you this.' Danes dropped a velvet purse (containing forty guineas) in the prince's hands. 'It is to defray the costs of sundries for my wife's purchases today. You may tell her that the more considerable bills may be sent home.'

'You do not give it to her yourself?'

'I do not. I neglected, on these first days of our marriage to notice my wife's state of dress, and also neglected the prompt giving of the pin money she is due.'

'I do not expect,' said the prince sympathetically, 'that you thought that a marquis's daughter would come to you so ill prepared.'

'I did not. It seems that you know rather more of my wife's situation than I do. Since I understand by your remark that you know of her stepmother, I should say that I do not take to the woman, but that she should shame the marquis by sending his daughter here so inappropriately dressed, and totally without funds, is beyond what I conceived of.'

'Hah! The marchioness is a villainess from a stage melodrama. She rather *ordered* the marquis to marry her. He, though my mother calls him a *dear creature*, is rather a weak person. His previous wife was somewhat domineering too, but she was beneficent in intention, rather than vicious. Little Eva was better dressed in those days, and happier, but I suppose she has grown a full two inches in the last four years which would account for the perfectly dreadful gown of last evening.'

'I think, though I do not pay attention to such things, that all her gowns may be dreadful. It is why I called you. If there are females to aid her today...'

'There is my mother the princess and my sister Gretchen, who is close to Eva's age. They were once great friends. My mother is English you know, so we spent a great deal of time here when young.'

'I see. In any case, Prince, you may ask your mother and sister to see to a suitable wardrobe for my wife, no expense need be spared.'

'That is very generous, especially if you knew how much my mother and sister can spend.'

'It is not generous. It is simply fitting to her position. I am known as rather a *warm* man.' Danes answered, referring indirectly to his vast wealth.

The prince grinned. 'So I understand. Well, and knowing this, Eva shall be transformed into the most fashionable of young ladies.'

'Very good,' said Danes, his face closing again. Then he recommenced. 'Are you in town for long, your highness?'

'We stay some months, I think.'

'Then might I ask that your mother and sister squire my wife to balls and Almacks and the like? I do not attend such occasions, and I believe that Lady Danes does not have much female acquaintance in town.'

'Certainly!' Prince Werther looked at the baronet in a manner that Danes found uncomfortably intrusive, as though trying to define his thoughts. 'You are a good man, Danes.'

'I hope I am not a bad one. But I am not a man given to female entertainments, and I realise that my wife is rather left adrift at times.'

'Yes. You would have expected that a girl of twenty might be rather more up to snuff than Eva. But she is a clever girl, she will learn her position quickly, and my Mama might give her some pointers too. I assure you she will make any man a good wife.'

Danes, his face still closed, said, 'I trust so. In any case, I shall come with you to greet the ladies before you go.'

They did so. The princess was sharp of feature, but kind of eye, and richly gowned. Her daughter — Gretchen, was it? — was grasping Eva's hand and swinging it, glad of the reunion, apparently. She was as fashionable, Danes thought, as his wife was dowdy. But his wife, he surprised himself by thinking, was prettier.

'What a dreadful gown,' Gretchen Starhemberg was saying in a reprise of her brother's comment on the brown silk of last evening. 'We shall burn it after today!'

'Shall we?' said Eva.

'Absolutely!' agreed the Princess, 'It must be banished.'

'It is quite warm, though.' said Eva.

'Then you might send it to a home for fallen woman to make them more respectable,' said the royal sister, shockingly.

Danes noted, as the party left the hall, that his wife was bright-eyed and a little vivacious. She seemed to speak to the prince in a tone of intimate raillery and asked after Ingrid. This, it appeared, was the name of the prince's wife, now in seclusion to await giving birth.

But looking from his study window Danes saw her in the carriage, and he realised that she had wandered off again in her thoughts, as though the excitable Starhembergs were dragging her through a pleasant dream, but she was not quite awake.

Danes wanted this whole thing dealt with … today. That is, the responsibility of having a wife who did not disgrace herself or him, and he had scrawled a list of things to do to achieve this. To this end he called her maid and gave instructions, called in the housekeeper, butler and cook and gave further instructions, and assembled the entire staff to reiterate their duties to Lady Danes.

He reminded the butler to ask his lady to see him before dinner this evening. The last and gravest worry about having a wife, or at least this wife, he would deal with then.

***

The lady's maid had told him that the dress had been altered by her ladyship herself the day that she had been informed of the dinner. It had been her only silk, and when her ladyship had first arrived, she had instructed it be laid aside as it was a relic of her grandmother. The maid looked shamefaced. 'I did not have the time to recut it when madam showed it to me, and I believed that she knew what she was about.'

'There is no need for my lady to be sewing or altering her garments. What do I pay *you* for?'

The maid, a middle-aged woman from his mama's time, looked crestfallen.

Danes looked grave. 'Never again. Her ladyship's appearance must always reflect my good name.'

During his interview with the butler, the man reported that his lady had given no orders to him, even for her own comfort, apart from the shawl when she sat in the hall on the second evening.

'You will invite her ladyship to tour the rooms and ask her how she wishes them disposed. All except my study. I care little what she does.' The butler bowed. 'And you may mention that anything she should wish to purchase for the house or change in the furnishings and linens may have the bills sent home.' The baronet sighed. 'The house has not had a lady in it for some time. Lady Danes should, at least, be able to look around her at things she likes, I suppose.'

'Yes, my lord.'

'If the Prince's party comes back with her, you might mention the furnishings before them. They will, perhaps help my wife in her choices. They are very fashionable.'

The housekeeper was instructed to report to his wife for orders each morning after breakfast, and the cook asked to do the same, after which she should simply send her menus for approval.

To the footmen and maids, the baronet made a speech about always serving his wife well.

'For example, my wife may have preferences in food, and is too well bred to mention it. I expect the footman to pay attention and to report it to cook. You must ask at every turn if there is anything further to make her comfortable.'

A little maid put up her hand. 'I think Her Ladyship be a little on the cold side, my lord, but she did not ask for coals.'

The butler looked his displeasure at her, and the girl blushed, but Danes said, 'Well observed. Then all rooms on the ground floor shall have fires lit, in case my lady should like to use them, and so too her bedchamber.'

'Yes, my lord,' said the butler.

'What is your name, girl?' Danes asked the maid who had spoken.

'Betty, my lord!'

'It seems that there are things Burke here does not have *time* for...' there was an audible groan from the lady's maid, 'so you will now be the assistant lady's maid to Burke.'

He dismissed them all coldly, and thought, 'There, it is done! Accommodating a wife in a gentlemanly fashion in only two hours!' He had completed the task thoroughly, after the dreadful dress had shaken him into a night's cogitation. He should have made some provisions for her comfort, but he had assumed that the daughter of a marquis would walk in and take charge on her own. But it was some years, the prince had told him, that she had been living under the repressive cloud of the new marchioness.

Once the final task was completed, he might see her as little as he had first judged fit. So, not at all.

***

Danes heard the commotion in the hallway that indicated the arrival of his wife with a great many boxes, and by the raised aristocratic voice of an elder female, he supposed the prince's party had come too.

'You must be exhausted, my lady, I shall send for refreshments.'

'What? Oh, thank you Bishop. Bring them to the green salon, perhaps.'

She sounded, thought Dane, still a little vague, but excited.

'Oh, the peach silk will arrive tomorrow, my dear,' said the lofty voice of the Princess, 'it will look divine on you!'

They chattered on and obviously left the hall, which now only rang with the steps of maids and footmen carrying packages to her chamber. Twenty minutes later, he was to conclude that the butler had done his job, for he heard the party of four tour the rooms, and then a chattering in the hall again.

'You must change the green salon, Eva. It is too dull by far,' said the younger royal personage.

'Well, but it is always called the *green salon*, you know,' said Eva, doubtfully.

Danes, listening, silently agreed.

But I suppose...' Danes listened intently, for his young wife seemed to be about to spout the first opinion of her own. '...it might be done in *sea green*. I saw silk in that colour which I loved but did not become me.'

'Sea green,' said the elder Princess, 'indeed. Just reupholster the chairs and have new drapes and then put the silk you liked on the walls and *voila!*'

'Elegant!' agreed the ladies.

'Well, well, you must all seek the silk drapers on your own tomorrow, for I am done.' said the prince in an exhausted tone.

'Oh no, my son. We need your decerning eye.'

'Is it really permissible to cause such upset in the house? And the cost...!' worried Eva.

'The cost?' The prince laughed. 'Your husband is one of the richest men in England, *Lady Danes*.'

'Is he...?' she asked, vague again.

'Yes,' said the younger Germanic voice, 'and I think he wishes his new wife to leave her touch on his home.'

He heard the prince say, in a mock solemn voice, Danes believed, 'It is your wifely duty.'

'Oh well, then,' his wife's voice sounded more enthusiastic. 'When shall we go shopping?'

'I think that...'

But Danes was not to hear what the princess thought, for the party moved out of the hall, but he was glad that his plan had gone aright. He left for his club before the Starhembergs had departed, feeling a sense of relief. The last step would be this evening, and then he would be done.

***

He arrived home before seven thirty, and said idly to the butler, who was receiving his hat and gloves, 'I'll dine with my wife this evening.'

'Her ladyship has gone out to dinner, my lord.'

'She has?' Danes was startled.

'The prince and his family took her for a light dinner before Almacks, I understand.'

'Ah!'

'Her ladyship looked charming this evening,' ventured the butler, moving the bread closer to the baronet's elbow.

'I did not ask you.'

'Pardon, my lord.'

So, the baronet had a solitary dinner at home, disgruntled at the first hitch in his one-day plan.

Danes debated whether he should await her arrival, and finish his appointed task, but as the clock struck midnight, he surrendered the notion of finishing it tonight, and went to bed. An evening at Almacks, he thought, could continue for a couple of hours yet.

It took him some time to get to sleep, irritated by the day's extension of the business of being a husband, which he wanted finished *today*. Then it awoke him ... a brush of lips on his cheek! He grasped her wrist with an iron fist, and she squealed. He sat upright like a jack-in-the-box. '*Never* enter my chamber!' he said with genuine rage.

'No, my lord.' her voice was choked.

'Never again!'

'Yes!' she said and tried to twist her hand away, looking at him piteously.

'Enough!' he said releasing her, ' I will speak to you at breakfast.'

She ran to the door with a rustle of silk, opened it softly and turned to breathe, 'Goodnight my lord.'

Danes lay back, incensed by both her presumption and her daring. And further incensed that her breathy goodnight had a softening effect on him. This piece of rage he reserved for himself.

***

At breakfast the next morning, the baronet looked at his apparently repentant wife. With a reticence born of the servants listening ears, he began, 'No repeat of last night must occur.'

'Oh no!' she looked quite frightened.

'After breakfast I shall speak to you further on this topic.'

'Very well.' There was a silence of three minutes after which she ventured, 'Thank you very much for the clothes. I'm afraid the princess ordered a great deal, some of which is still being made up. I did not think I needed quite so much, but Gretchen said that I needed to dress well for your prestige.'

'Indeed. There is no need for gratitude.'

'But still, I am very grateful,' she said in a small voice. He nodded and there was another long pause while they ate silently.

'What did you decide to do about the rooms downstairs?' he enquired casually.

'Oh, the princess said that the Chinese room is perfect as it is for formal visits. She says the carpets alone must have cost a king's ransom.'

'They did,' remarked Danes eyes still on his meat.

'And I like the yellow salon, but Gretchen said the hangings are faded, which is true. It might be difficult to match the upholstery fabric, so I propose to go a shade darker with the curtains, perhaps with gold. It should not then require reupholstery and such botheration. If that is agreeable to you, my lord.'

'You may do as you wish in your own home, my lady.'

'What a novel thought!' she said, amazed, 'I have not done as I wished for a long time.'

He was silent. He did not want to exchange confidences with her.

'The rest of the rooms are perfectly appointed, but I may move the seating and so on to make it cosier.'

For whom, he thought, would it need be cosy? He remained silent.

'Do you like my new gown?' she suddenly asked. 'Gretchen insisted I try it on. We were lucky that the model in the dressmakers was my size.'

He looked at the sheer French muslin made up to the neck, the sleeves a little puff. It was in primrose, with some sort of figuring, and it looked ... 'It is quite suitable,' he said flatly.

She smiled at him then, and he lowered his eyes, ducking the power of it. He had meant to come here to scold her, not receive her gratitude, say words of admiration, exchange confidences, or any other such intimacy. Well, the scold would begin now. The distance must be kept. He gestured the servants from the room, whispering to Bishop as he did so.

They were alone. She gazed up at him timidly.

'I will not eat you,' he said, annoyed.

'No, my lord,' she began a smile, which further annoyed him, so he frowned her down.

'I will reiterate what I said last night. *Never again!* This house is large. You may make any arrangements you choose in the other rooms, but my study and bedchamber are sacrosanct. Do you understand?'

'Yes.'

'My country home, Boston Park, is larger still. There you may also do as you wish, change whatever you wish, since you are Lady Danes. However, my study, bedchamber and library are my own and must never be breached.'

'I am forbidden the library?' she said, a little dejected.

'Are you fond of books?'

'Very.'

'Then you might enter every Monday between nine o'clock and ten to find what you will. There are few novels there, however. It is better you attend Hatchards before you leave London and order what suits you.'

'You are too kind, my lord.'

'It is not kindness. I wish my wife to be fully empowered to see to her own comforts and amusements without disturbing me.'

'I see,' she cast her eyes down again.

'About ...' here he paused, 'your oath.' He looked up and she blushed. 'I see that you are stubborn on this point so I shall permit the insanity. Look up!' she did so, timidly. 'You may come before dinner each evening and perform the deed ...' he blanched as he said it, 'on this part of my cheek only. He held his thumb and forefinger an inch apart midway between his ear and mouth, 'in this area only.'

'On just that side?' she enquired.

'On whatever side presents itself, but only there, do you hear me? And only then. I do not want a human bullet shooting at me from the dark corners of hall or corridors in my house.'

'What,' she considered head to one side, 'if you are in your study before I dine?'

'Then you may come in after knocking. You have a half minute to leave.'

'If you are in your bedchamber?' She saw his frown and said, 'I am just covering every eventuality.'

'Then you must wait until I leave my bedchamber.'

'What if I am to dine out?'

'Then you will do so before you leave.' He frowned, recalling that he had been gone when she left. 'If you have a plan to dine out, inform the butler at the earliest, and I shall let him know when it is convenient.'

'That would not really be in the spirit of the oath. We may have to kiss at ten in the morning some days.'

'It is the best I can do to accommodate you, madam. Do not push me.'

'I quite see that, and I am grateful. Trapping you was a little exhausting.' she added reflectively.

'For both of us.' He stood up. 'I shall ride now. I trust you have a pleasant day, my lady.'

Though this was said somewhat coldly, she smiled as she gave her response.

'It will be so pleasant now that I do not have to worry about the oath.'

He paused at the door, as though he had just thought of something. 'Do you ride?' Again, the cold tone.

'A little. I have not done so often these three years.' he supposed she meant since the time of her dreadful stepmama. 'I used to drive too.'

He nodded and left. The butler, after she had freshened up, ready for another shopping spree with the Starhembergs, told her the head groom was awaiting her in the green salon.

This individual stood in his stocking feet, looking somewhat awkward to be indoors, Eva thought. She waited.

The baronet had called him the man said, to enquire into what kind of horse his mistress would like him to find for her. And would she like a quiet pair for a curricle?

Eva, at a loss, and nodding, was thankful that the prince's family arrived during this interval, and His Highness told the groom that his mistress was belittling her skill, that he personally would choose a mare and a pair for her and send the bill to the baronet.

'Your husband is belatedly attentive,' remarked the old princess.

'I have only been married five days!' protested Eva.

'He expected Eva to come better prepared and know how to take charge, I believe,' remarked the prince.

Gretchen took this up, 'And no one could have thought that you were out for *three years* and did not possess an evening gown.'

Eva sighed, but it seemed quite amusing from this distance. The distance her marriage had gleaned her.

'The marchioness did not think my manners *polished enough* for evening society, though I was allowed to attend some afternoon entertainments. She complained that I had no *prospects,* as she called them, or gentlemen callers, but how I was to have such when I did not go out at night, I could hardly tell. But she said so to anyone who would listen.'

'My dear, if I thought that things were so bad, I should have kidnapped you to my Schloss!' said the old princess, taking Eva's hand.

'I did not think the marquis would allow...' began Gretchen.

'Oh, Papa does not always notice things,' explained Eva, 'And then ... he is so very *terrified* of her, it is almost amusing.'

'And you were not?' asked Prince Werther.

'Not really. Afraid of the scenes she made, a lot of the time. That was humiliating, so I did my best never to go against her. But she is too ridiculous to really *hurt* me,' she had tilted her chin up as she said so in a manner her friends admired and felt sad about at once. 'It was just not ... *happy* after she joined the family.'

'Well,' said Prince Werther in a bracing tone, 'you may be happy forthwith, with the backing of your rich baronet.'

'Indeed!' Eva said, as brightly as she could.

'He is rather serious, I think,' remarked Gretchen, 'but so very handsome!'

This morning at least, she was more relaxed. Her husband's compromise about the oath had pleased and somewhat amused her. It had surprised her, too. So much had happened yesterday, and she had so much bounty to thank him for, and the visits from the upper servants this morning had shown her how to get along more as Lady Danes, mistress of this house. She would learn to assume her position so as to give him as little worry as possible.

Her new freedom she owed to him, and she was grateful. From the first, he had issued orders and restrictions, but his coldness had somehow not penetrated her. He left her to her own devices and had not interfered or enquired when she went out to visit her cousin or took a maid for a walk in the park. She had met a friend of her father's there once and he and his wife had called her, most respectfully, Lady Danes. She had been able to visit places of interest even in those early days. On one delicious afternoon she had purchased a novel in Hatchards and then visited a tearoom, with only her maid present, and read there. All this was a result of being Lady Danes, a married lady, not Lady Eva, daughter of a marquis and a harridan of a stepmama.

She had been a little afraid of him at first, and thus preparing to live behind the vagueness she had learned from her papa as a shield. But somehow, even when Sir Rupert had frowned horribly at her, she had checked on her feelings afterwards and had felt herself unwounded. Why his frowns and coldness were not as damaging to her as they should have been, she could not really say. But lying in bed last night she had thought of a theory. His coldness, like Papa's vagueness, was assumed, and for the same purpose perhaps — protection. This contrasted with her stepmother's venom, which came from the core of her.

She had worn pink silk last night and had quite agreed with her prince when he said she looked pretty. Unfortunately, the marchioness and Abigail were missing from Almacks, for she would have liked to have seen Abigail be jealous of a dress she could not be permitted to wear (since she was unmarried), and the marchioness furious.

She had guessed that as well as the financial gains for the impoverished marquis (for Papa was hopeless at running his estates) the marchioness had seen Danes' stone face and stern demeanour and had hoped that he would make Eva a cruel husband. But it was not so, he was just a disinterested one. But then she thought about the visit by the groom, when Danes had just realised that he had not provided for her stabling needs, and she concluded that the baronet was not *completely* disinterested. He was nicer than he pretended to be.

But he did not wish her to coax him towards her, and so she would not. She would perform her oath quickly and surgically, so as not to bother him, and keep out of his way like the wife he wished for.

Last night, she had very much enjoyed her first ball, wearing the right thing, and among friends. She had been introduced to *everyone* it seemed, for the princess had a large acquaintance. She listened to Gretchen's chatter about suitors and joined in the comparisons about those eligible gentlemen who had asked the pretty blonde to dance. She knew a quick pang that she had never had her chance to deal with suitors, or the freedom to choose her favourites, and she wondered if she might have encouraged Danes if he had approached her in this environment. If he asked her to dance on a night such as this, she would have been flattered, for although his was a very serious face, the long bones and blue eyes were distinctly handsome, and he was, moreover, *extremely* eligible. This, in London phraseology, simply meant wealthy and of good breeding — both of which qualifications he amply met. She had been lucky to be his practical choice for a wife, though, and she killed the romantic notions that Gretchen displayed in her hearing, with a heavy stone.

It was, moreover, when talking, laughing and dancing amongst the glittering throng, impossible not to know how very lucky she was.

***

Danes informed his wife, through the butler, that she was to accompany him to another political dinner, and the butler let him know that her ladyship had cancelled a previous appointment to do so. Danes nodded.

On the evening of the joint breakfast his little wife had knocked the study door at seven o'clock, entered at his grunt, come behind his desk, kissed the relevant spot lightly, said 'Goodnight, my lord,' and had run off obediently. He had sat ramrod stiff since her knock, and endured it well, sighing as she left. If this was all it was, he could bear with it.

When he had gone to sleep, he was glad to know that he had not thought too much of the incident for the rest of the evening, as the previous insults to his person had caused him to do on the previous occasions. He had made the commission of her insane oath bearable.

On the next evening, she had entered the green salon. She came, kissed and was gone in a flash, and he sighed again. He had not been so tense either, he had not even looked up from his book. It might be better, he reflected, if he was generally in the green salon at the appointed hour, for he still felt her intrusion into the study.

On the third evening he had almost forgotten her oath, for his friend Frederick Bailey had come to drive him to his club. Bailey and another two friends who accompanied him, had wished to see his new wife, but Danes was steering them out when Eva, who must have been in the green salon, came out and, before them all, kissed his cheek and said, 'Good night, My Lord!' before she had smiled, cheeks rouged, at his companions, who bowed and spoke to her. She only ran from them, after giving him a beat to introduce them, which he could not do after the shock of being kissed in public.

'A pretty, affectionate little wife you have there, Danes, but adorably shy,' remarked Frederick Bailey. 'I thought you would choose a cool, reserved beauty more like yourself. But ... whyever did you not introduce us?'

'Next time, gentlemen,' said Danes, 'next time. I shall invite you to dinner, to be properly introduced.' He realised, through his shock, that this was another of the normalities that he must do, introduce his wife to his friends, those beyond political circles. Being married, he thought, in the middle of his lingering confusion at being kissed in front of his friends, was more work than he had planned for. 'You may bring your wives or family members, for my wife does not as yet have much acquaintance in town.'

Montague said, 'Does she always kiss you goodnight?'

'Every night.' Danes said, and somehow, he felt ... could it be ... *proud?*

'Ah well, it is early days for you. My wife is as liable to throw a spoon at me as kiss me these days,' said Potter, sadly.

'Let us go before the best tables are taken at Watier's,' said Danes a trifle smugly, marshalling them out of the hall.

***

On the night of the political dinner, Danes came downstairs to see his wife in the same velvet evening cape and gauze shawl on her head, but asked her to part the cape, so that he might see her dress. It was cream satin with brown velvet ribbons under her bosom, and a brown velvet rose at her decollete. His breath halted a moment, but he nodded cool approval and they moved on.

***

It was quite a large party, with a dinner table that took up almost all of the dining room's grand length. It was the home of Mrs Manton, a famous political hostess, Danes had told her in the carriage. They were to celebrate the passing of a bill through parliament, but Eva had glazed over and did not now remember which bill. It was a party of verve and intelligent discussion, though she was sandwiched between two of the dullest of the gentlemen present, which suited her mood. She could not imagine taking part in the political debate and felt inadequate somewhat. However, she gazed around the table, admired the ladies' gowns — while happily feeling no inferiority of her own. She stirred herself to note names and characteristics of the gentlemen present, for no doubt she might meet them again, and it would be her job to recognise them politely, for her husband's sake. This proved an entertainment for her.

The most interesting aspect of the evening had been the time when the ladies sat in the drawing room while the gentlemen lingered in the dining room over their port.

'I did not think Danes would have wed so young a wife! How long has it been, my Lady?' It was Lady Helena Carter, a very fashionable lady in her forties, with dark hair and humorous eyes. Her husband Baron Carter had been one of the wits at the table.

This was said in the intrusive but warm manner of her friend the prince, and so Eva was able to smile and say, 'Almost two weeks only.'

'Have you been to many of these tedious affairs since then?'

'Only tonight, and at the Von Bergers last week. But I met my prince there, so it was not dull at all.'

'Your prince?' said a croaked but languid voice from the side, belonging to a pigeon-breasted dame of fifty dressed in claret velvet, 'you do not hold your *husband* as your prince, but choose another?'

Eva blushed, but her sophisticated companion, Lady Carter, said in her stead, 'If it was the Von Berger's, she must mean Prince Werther Starhemberg,' she smiled. 'Did I guess aright?'

'Yes,' Eva said, 'he and I are family friends.'

'I did not see you much in town, Lady Danes. Did Sir Rupert catch you when you were just out?' This was said by a lady in a blue dress, richly adorned by embroidered roses, with blue silk roses in her hair. The tone was sarcastic and ill-intentioned, Eva thought, and wondered why. But then some people, like her stepmama, were just disposed to make others uncomfortable.

But there was no need to allow *this* lady to do so, so she replied, a little coolly. 'I have been out three years, but I did not attend many evening functions.'

The bored voice from the fire seat said, 'What is the point of being *out* if one does not attend evening events?'

Eva's tone remained cool, her eyes just flicking towards the red velvet briefly, 'You would have to ask my stepmother.'

'And *still,* you married the richest man in town!' exclaimed the lady in the blue gown with continued venom, 'How *did* you manage it?' The look which she gave Eva seemed to doubt the qualifications of her charms.

This woman was called ... what was it? ... Eva's voice dropped another degree in response, 'There was a childhood arrangement between the families, I understand.'

'A betrothal arrangement of *long standing*?' Here the lady actually *scoffed*, '... which the young Lord Danes ignored long enough to become engaged to *me*.'

A hush fell upon the room, and Eva was deprived of air. But her companion, Lady Helena, said, after a beat, 'And which *you* then ignored, Valentine, to run off with the earl.'

Countess Roberts, that is how she had been introduced, thought Eva. The earl was the dull man seated next to Eva at dinner. She had made a slight jest at him, and the earl had finally got it a full ten seconds later, and said, 'Very good, very good!' She had seen the blue gowned lady look over at his laugh. Jealous or embarrassed by his lugubrious chortle? Eva had not been able to guess.

Eva now looked over at Danes' once-betrothed and smiled, turning to her companion saying, a trifle under her breath, 'And it seems she rues her choice.'

Lady Helena grinned. Another lady, who had overheard, laughed aloud, and Valentine, the pretty Countess Roberts, called, '*What* did you say?' The other chattering ladies stopped all conversation, for the countess had a raised voice.

She might have been pretty, reflected Eva, if her face did not wear such unpleasant expressions.

'Merely wondered if you rued your choice, my lady,' Eva said, facing the countess squarely.

EUPHEMIA AND THE UNEXPECTED ENCHANT... 125

'How *dare* you?' that woman spat.

'How dared *you* leave a good man like my husband to the ridicule of the polite world?' returned Eva.

Lady Carter raised her brows. Clearly there was more to this young lady than she had thought.

Everyone looked to the countess, remembering the old scandal, and wondering what her response would be.

'Daphne,' said Lady Helena to another lady, in a voice that ignored the drama, 'might you join us and give us your opinion on our new wife's future reading material?'

Lady Daphne, a young wife of a handsome MP whose name Eva had forgotten, came forward and sat on the other side of the gilt legged sofa and said, 'Oh I do not think she must be forced to read *much* do you?'

'I agree. Most husbands do not like a managing, knowing female, but use us as respite from political cares. However, it does one no good to appear an idiot, like Lucy here,' Lady Helena gestured to a pretty young girl who had seemed the most bored all evening, 'who only reads the fashion pages of journals.'

'I say!' complained Lucy, Mrs Marsden, whose tawny good looks Eva had admired. 'When I just gave you that recipe for Denmark Water, too!'

'Yes, Mrs Marsden keeps us all up to the mark, and you must call on her if you wish to shop. She has wonderful taste...' Lucy Marsden smiled at this, '... but no brain at all.' Lady Helena concluded sadly. Mrs Marden's face fell.

The elder lady in red velvet came forward and gestured Lucy from her chair, sat and said, in the cracked, bored tone habitual to her, 'That is quite true, Lady Helena. But might I remind you that you are *far* too dedicated to the truth for a *politician's* wife.' The lady turned to

Eva, the rubies above her red velvet sparkling as she did so, 'What I suggest, Lady Danes, is that you read the first page of all the journals in the morning and at least try to acquaint yourself with *names*. Then, if someone were to ask, *what is your opinion on Lord Archer's remarks in the house yesterday?* you might answer, *I have not yet read his speech, but I look forward to the foreign secretary's measured response,* which shows you know who he *is*, at least.' This seemed like a great deal for the bored socialite to say, and Eva smiled an ironic response. She remembered that this lady was Viscountess Belcher, wife of a cabinet minister, The woman, in order to be seated here, had had to pass Countess Roberts, who now stood, rather isolated, by the fire.

'Yes dear,' agreed Lady Helena. 'The good thing, and the bad thing all at once, is that Danes will no doubt take you to *many* such occasions and you will soon be able to put faces to the names that you con from the papers.'

Eva smiled and was warmed by the pleasantries, but she still smarted about the beautiful lady standing by the fire. How *dare* she? Was that the kind of female her husband admired when he had chosen for himself? Dark and lovely, with a hard mouth and a charming profile? Eva was glad for his sake that he had avoided that marriage, for, even if his youthful heart had not known it then, she was a cat. A jealous cat, to boot. Her heart contracted for him. In the melee when the gentlemen returned to take tea before departure, Eva touched Lady Helena's arm to recall her attention.

'If I might ask, Lady Helena,' she said in a low voice, 'how long ago was that broken engagement?'

'I do not know ...' she mused, '... perhaps ten years since. Yes, it was my first Season's scandal. Danes is well out of *that* connection. The countess leads her husband a pretty dance, you know.'

Eva nodded.

'I do not usually breathe scandal, but you are as well to be aware that Valentine may henceforth mean you harm. I'll call tomorrow after breakfast and take you up for a ride around the park. I will say as much as I can to you of your reserved husband, but it will not be much. Or will you feel me intrusive?'

'Not at all. You have stood my friend tonight, and I would love to pursue the acquaintance.'

'Oh, there are many more dull dinners when we will meet again, fear not. But I shall call tomorrow anyway.'

***

On the carriage ride home, Danes was aware that his silent wife was stealing glances at him, and it made him feel uncomfortable. He did not wish to raise the subject, however, so he did not speak. But, as the carriage bowled around the square, she shifted her seat to sit at his side, rather than opposite him, and took his face between her hands, which made him stiffen. But they had not as yet fulfilled her oath, so he stayed still. By the light of the flickering lantern inside, he saw her face, serious and full of emotion, tears welling in her luminous eyes.

'What are you about?' he said in horror.

She parted the fingers on the right side of his face to give access to the prescribed area and kissed his cheek, but somewhat lingeringly. 'Goodnight, my lord,' she breathed in a choked voice. For a second, he looked into those glittering eyes, seeing a tear fall. Her hands were still on his cheeks and somehow, he was too spellbound to jerk away. The carriage had stopped, she whisked herself out and into the house before he could reply.

He sat in the carriage for a moment, trying to get his bearings.

***

The next morning, he met Helena Carter coming in as he was going out, and he gestured her into his study and asked, 'Something I did not see happened last night, Lady Helena. What was it?'

'It was Valentine, The Countess of Malice. She was a foul vixen, and now Lady Danes knows of your previous engagement.'

'Was my wife insulted?' he asked, now in a rage.

'No, Sir Rupert, it was *your wife* who insulted the *countess*. Very efficiently.'

'My wife?'

'Yes, your little wife, who looks like she would not say boo to a goose told the countess, when she taunted her with your previous engagement, and I then chided her back relating the scandal — that Valentine appeared to *rue her decision.*'

Danes gave a shout of laughter, holding himself afoot by leaning on his desk, 'She said *that?*'

Lady Helena, who had not seen so natural a laugh from Danes since her first Season, thought to add fuel. 'She did. And then, when Valentine asked her how she dared speaks thus, Lady Danes retaliated by asking how dared Valentine leave *a good man like her husband* to face the world's derision? She was perfectly marvellous!'

Danes stood, puffing out his chest.

Lady Helena saw it, amused. Again, she added fuel.

'She is very pretty, your wife. And not stupid. And so *furious* in defence of you last evening.'

Danes nodded, a slight smile at the corner of his mouth which his friend watched in amusement. But she warned, 'Watch out that Valentine does her no harm in Town.'

He nodded again, but still smiling. He wore it all day, that smile. He thought of many things, and about the preposterousness of his present situation. This amused him too — he found himself amused by almost everything today. A maid's dishevelled cap, a clumsy footman dropping a fork. A dog's antics in the park. It all made him smile.

His wife came in sometime in the afternoon, but he awaited with bated breath the hour before dinner. She came into his study at seven o'clock, rushed to him and bent down for the oath's fulfilment. In a magical stroke of timing, he turned his face, and her lips landed on his, if a trifle to one side. She jerked back, but he was on his feet and had taken her by the waist of her stylish sprigged muslin, and looked down into those large shocked brown eyes before he kissed her again.

Even when he stopped, she was breathing heavily, the ability to speak suspended, and he said, still holding her waist, 'Your grandfather was right, a kiss before bedtime cures all ills.'

'My lord...!' she said, shaken. But he was avidly watching for signs of disgust, and he could see none.

'Were you *very* sorry for me last night, when your eyes looked such love at me in the carriage?'

'I ...!'

'She is nothing to me now,' he said, his words a caress, his eyes on her lips.

'But she *hurt* you.' Her shy hand stole to his cheek.

He grasped it and held it there in his own strong hand. 'Yes. I was only a boy and I thought I would die of it. I was wrong. She only made me desert my feelings, but since you came ...!' He sighed a giant sigh. 'Can you accept my feelings, Lady Danes? It is late, I know.'

'Only by two weeks. Today is the fourteenth day.'

'But *can* you...?'

'If you do not let me go, I suppose I have no choice.' She smiled at him, and he smiled back broadly.

'We shall be so happy!' his voice like a boy's, full of enthusiasm. Perhaps it was the voice of the young gentleman who had been so wounded ten years ago. 'I do not know when it started, but I suspect that your first kiss was like an axe on the ice around my heart.'

'Grandpapa was wiser than I thought. *And* in choosing you as my husband.'

'Did I make you very afraid of me? I was so *cruel* to you.' The boyish admission made her smile, it was so unlike her cold, chiding husband. He hugged her closer then sat again and pulled her onto his lap.

'The chair arms attack me!' she complained, and then he carried her bodily to a small sofa near a bookcase. 'Hug me close,' she required of him delightfully, 'This is the only room without a fire now.' He did hug her, covering one bare arm with one of his own and tucking her into his coat.

'This is so comfortable,' he said, in a happy daze. 'This will be my *life* from now on!'

'In a room with a fire only,' she teased. 'But to answer you, I never mistook you for cruel, for I have lived with a truly cruel person. You were unlike my Papa, I thought, for you were trying to control your life and succeeding, but without harm to others. I think I always knew that you were a hurt person, for only the hurt fear intimacy as much as you. I rather enjoyed your fear of *me*, you know.'

'A wicked woman.' He sighed. 'I should just tell you, and I know it is too soon for you, but I have fallen completely in love for the second time in my life.'

'Oh, goodness! I think *I* have too — no, I am sure of it! When Gretchen was drooling over her suitors at Almacks, I briefly thought that it would have been nice to have a free choice of eligible gentlemen as she has, but I soon thought, that if *you* had asked me to dance on such an occasion, I should *always* choose you. I like your face, and your seriousness, and the way you were always so honest with me, when I had been living so long with duplicity. It restored me to myself. To the time before Mama died.'

'I'm glad. But I fear for the seriousness you admire. I have been grinning all day since Lady Helena told me of the events of last night. Of your brave championing of me.'

'*That?* That was nothing! That woman is a rude, irrelevant creature.'

She was haughty, as became his bride, but he saw her look her anger and he kissed the top of her head. '*Darling,*' he said.

She tipped the head against his chest and looked up at him. '*What* did you call me?'

'Darling. What would you prefer? Sweetheart, My Own, *Dearest* …?'

'Stop, stop,' she laughed, 'this is all too sudden! Last evening my husband was reluctant to *touch* me and now he fastens me so tight I can barely breathe …' she smiled at him, her eyes glazed with happy tears, '… but I like it best when you call me *Lady Danes*. It was Lady Danes, backed by all your generosity to me, that spoke last night. I fear *nothing* as long as I am Lady Danes,' her husband hugged her tighter at this, making her squeal. Her voice became low, and she grasped at his waistcoat, 'But sometime, I would like to hear my given name from you…' she tailed off, shyly.

'And mine from you. Tonight then, in my chamber!' he breathed in her ear.

She sat up then and pulled away. 'I am afraid, Your Lordship, that I am forbidden your chamber on pain of death.'

He pulled her back and kissed her neck which made her giggle. 'My lady…' he pleaded, '*Lady Danes…*' he added for good measure.

'It appears,' she said wryly, 'that there is one thing Lady Danes fears. That is, *you*, my lord.'

She stood up and smiled and held out a hand to him. 'I'm hungry!' she said, in a pleading tone.

'Let us to dinner!' he took her hand through his arm and made his way with her to the dining room. The hall servants looked aghast, some with open jaws.

Lady Danes paused at a footman. 'Oh John, send a message to the Prince Werther's family that I shall stay at home tonight, and visit tomorrow, perhaps.'

'Late afternoon!' added the baronet, which for some reason made her ladyship blush and look scoldingly at him, but they smiled at each other and walked on.

The baronet had *smiled*! Jaws dropped, but the butler was thankfully too engaged in holding open the dining room door to notice this break in their rigorous training in reserve.

'What happened there, then?' said the first footman, shocked.

'Can you not see that our master is in love?' scoffed another.

'But he's ... grinning.'

'I knew that l'il fox would have him,' said the first footman, who had worked here under the last baronet also. 'Good on 'er! It's these ten years I haven't seen that smile.'

'Well, I never!' said the shocked younger footman.

'Get along with your message! We don't want no one disturbing our master and mistress this evening!'

The man was gone and the first footman, in a stately manner, received a tray from a kitchen maid, and went into the dining room for a better look. Two maids used him as a shield and peaked behind his head to see the diners sitting closer together than was seemly.

'In a few days, their master was saying, 'let us visit your stepmama.

'Must we?' said her ladyship plaintively.

'Certainly!' her husband replied firmly. 'I will send for the family jewels, and you will wear every trinket you can, as well as your best dress.

'How vulgar!' she remarked, amused.

'Extremely! But the marchioness will be jealous to the core!'

'And so will Abigail!' She replied with relish.'

'Yes. Let me be unpleasant to her for you, as you were for me last night.'

'Oooh ...!' said her ladyship enjoying this thought, 'use your *cold* voice, it used to make me quake in my boots

'*Darling!*' he apologised, holding her hand, 'but I shall be more than cold, I shall be *deadly.*'

'Well and so you may, sometime. But dearest, might we not just treasure our happiness a while yet? I will not let her spoil my joy.'

'My wife is wise as well as beautiful!' Danes said, caressing her cheek

The servants exchanged looks, dumbfounded at the swift and total change in their master.

***

'It were all the kisses that done it! ' said little Betty in the kitchen later that evening. 'She bested him with them kisses!' for the staff had talked of little else below stairs than the various kiss sightings.

The butler, also shocked, lowered himself to nod in agreement. He smiled, remembering his lord's last order of the evening.

'See that I am not roused in the morning, Wilson. I will ring when I arise.' It was said in a casual tone, but his lord had flushed somewhat as he used to as a younger man, and he had not been able to prevent a smile playing on his lips.

Wilson had remained stone, but he had been glad, glad of the victory of the stolen kisses. His lord and lady mounted the stairs, he grasping her hand through his arm as though she might escape. But his lady dropped a head on his lordship's shoulder, needing the closeness as much as he, thought the watching butler.

Then she giggled and reached to kiss his cheek, as always. 'Goodnight, my lord!' she whispered, and his master had run the rest of the way with her, laughing.

Chapter Ten

Annis and the Grand Plan

Lady Blackwood had endured the kisses and demands of her offspring for twenty minutes and now, with her cherubs safely disposed with the nurse, she was able to breakfast with her husband -- who was at the other side of the table, reading correspondence -- in relative peace.

'I have a Grand Plan!' she informed him.

'Only 500 to those funds, mind, Short! Risky...'

A man standing behind the table made a note. 'Yes, my lord.'

'Can we not even *breakfast* without Short?' his wife complained, 'I am not dressed.'

Mr Short became a stone, but her husband glanced up the table, taking in the curls pulled under a cap, her pleated linen nightwear and her peignoir to her neck. 'You are wearing more clothes than usual,' he remarked.

'My lord!'

'Oh, leave us, Short!'

The man bowed and did so.

'I have a Grand Plan, I say,' her ladyship recommenced.

'Mmmm!' her husband replied, now reading a journal, turning in his chair to cross his legs.

She sent him a fuming glance, but it was fruitless, since he did not look her way. 'Do you not even wish me to say?'

'You have told me. You are bringing Miss Fleur Caldicott to meet Gaston and you are sure they will make a match of it since she is the only female he has ever complimented in your presence.' He added sardonically, 'in all his twenty-four years.

'It is time he wed. Think of the succession!' said Lady Blackwood, commandingly.

'I do,' replied her husband, unmoved. 'Because you mention it frequently. Must you meddle? Viscount Stanton can take care of his own marriage arrangements, or Trinity can. He *was* Gaston's guardian, after all.'

'Felix? *Fine* guardian! Gaston would have met *no one* in town if it had not been for me.'

'He met *many* people at his club, but I expect you mean young ladies.' Blackwood continued to eat, informing her, 'Felix couldn't introduce him to ladies, because he does not know any.'

'He must know their *mamas*, at least. He must have at least *danced* with women in his youth.'

'Not that I remember,' said Blackwood with effort. 'But perhaps some. His mother had your managing disposition, and she dragged him to Almacks and so on,' he waved his fork in demonstration, having recently speared a roll, '... but it did not take. *Felix* ...,' Baron Blackwood added with dry meaning, '... escaped captivity.'

'*What* did you say?' said the furious voice of his wife.

'Wedded bliss,' explained Blackwood, returning to his blood pudding.

Lady Blackwood ate something resentfully. But her husband merely finished breakfast and returned to the journal. Her resentment was not stronger than her need to share her genius, however, so after a moment she said, 'I have also had the *brilliant* notion of asking Annis Fallow to join us.'

'*What?*' Blackwood finally looked up.

'You know she has always been my *dearest* friend.'

'I know no such thing.'

'Well, she has! We were brought out in the same Season, and though she has been caring for her stepmother these last years, the old lady is now deceased, and Annis has come back to town. So, I thought that she could come to Trinity Manor and very likely make a match with Felix. She was a great friend of the two of you, was she not?'

'Somewhat. She was the child of a neighbour. She is six years Felix's junior.'

'So, you two never considered her as *a woman* then? I must be grateful that *I* was two years older, dearest.'

'Mmm. I do not think much of your Grand Plan.'

'Well, you need not concern yourself. At least I am making a push to help your relatives make good matches.'

His snap of the journal was the only thing that displayed a reaction after his first exclamation. Lady Blackwood had been regarding him narrowly.

'Do your worst, my dear,' he said, in his habitual indifferent tone. 'You usually do.'

***

Annis Fallow had been surprised, but hardly shocked, at being greeted as an old friend by Marjorie, Lady Blackwood. They had not previously been close, but in their first Season, since their Mamas had been friends, Annis had been often in her company. She watched as Marjorie won the heart of Baron Gilbert Blackwood, who had been a friend and a secret crush of Annis. She had looked upon him too long on one occasion, and that had set Marjorie's eye upon him too -- for Sir John Noble, whom Marjorie Ward admired, had danced with Annis *first* that evening.

Pretty Marjorie had followed the dance that she had so heavily hinted for when introduced to Gilbert, by a strong pursuit. This had included a dropped handkerchief, a twisted ankle, a bout of tears at some cruel intention *said she* (of Marjorie's own Mama, who was in fact, tremendously kind) to make her marry a rich cad, and finally, a fainting fit at a ball.

Annis had watched, amazed, as Gilbert, at first uninterested, had been seduced by these tactics, taking Marjorie's string of misfortunes as genuine. His behaviour, in saving her so often from manufactured calamity, had given rise to talk, and Gilbert had finally offered for her.

In later years Annis thought of the dance with Sir John Noble that had made Marjorie take her revenge, and wondered at the trifles that important life decisions may hang upon. When Annis had wished Gilbert happy, there had been a moment when his eyes changed as he had heard her trembling voice, and he suddenly looked as though some *great thing* had just occurred to him. It had not brought comfort to remember this afterwards, but only pain. It was too late for everyone.

But that was long ago.

Now Marjorie had invited her to Trinity, home of Gilbert's cousin Felix and his nephew Gaston, Viscount Stanton -- and Annis had decided, after all, to go. She was an independent lady of thirty-six, past any notion of marriage now, and she and Felix Trinity had once been friends. He would be forty-two, now, she believed. An old man! Annis was unafraid of being influenced by any scheme of Marjorie Blackwood's (and Felix, never would have been, she believed) -- but she would like to see him again, and to visit her old district, too. Some cousins lived at her old home, Fallow Manor, now, but there had been no falling out, or despicable behaviour between them at all. Annis was sure that Chester Fallow would have provided for her stepmother and she in case of indigence, but in fact Annis had inherited a comfortable property by the sea at Brighton from her grandmother, and another cosy town house in Bath.

Annis was neat and handsome, if not pretty (she had not considered herself so, even in her youth), with some wonderful russet curls and rather too many freckles. Her years by the sea in the Brighton house had not improved her complexion and no amount of cucumber water could fully erase the blight. But she had reached the age where such things need not concern her. Indeed, seeing the behaviour of young ladies in Town that Season, she had been reminded of those who were competitive (like Marjorie) and those who had been crippled by shyness (herself). Both personalities were anxious, the wisdom of age informed her, and she was not sorry that she now attended functions merely for the mere pleasure of meeting old friends.

Marjorie's presence was a trial, but one she could bear, since Gilbert would not attend, his wife had told Annis. Gilbert would remain in London.

***

'Why is the place in turmoil?' Viscount Stanton, a tall athletic youth wearing riding clothes said, as he entered the salon.

'I told Mrs Franklin that Lady Blackwood pays us a visit,' Felix Trinity said, not looking up from his book.

'Uncle Felix...!' Gaston Saunders, the viscount, said reproving. From the scale of the arrangements, his cousin's wife was not making an afternoon call. 'Why does she come here? Gilbert has a perfectly good house at the other end of the county.'

'I *claimed* we were busy, but Marjorie does not take a hint,' said Felix Trinity with a lack of interest.

'Why Uncle Gilbert ever married —!' Gaston complained.

'Be careful,' said Trinity, but bored.

'Oh well, since there's no hope for it, I'll just have to hunt at Pogo's a good deal,' said the young man with insouciance. 'And *you* shall entertain her!' Gaston added with relish.

'Really?' said the disinterested voice behind the book. 'Then there will be consequences.'

'I am six-and-twenty now Uncle Felix, not the child you took in. You can no longer offer me punishing consequences!' It was said with bravado, but Felix Trinity said nothing. After a time, Gaston asked, a trifle anxiously. 'What *will* you do?'

'I shall take my time in deciding!'

'Felix!'

'You used to whine like that for extra cake. You only have to entertain her. Invite your friends over if you cannot bear it. She may bring someone too.'

'Who?' said Gaston suspiciously. Behind the pages of the book, the viscount could swear that he *heard* his uncle grin.

***

Lady Blackwood's party arrived on Thursday evening, and Felix roused himself from the book room with a sigh at the announcement by the butler Rhodes, a stout man who looked like he consumed too much of the kitchen's supplies. Ladies were engaged in taking off bonnets and pelisses and giving them to the waiting servants and Lady

Marjorie Blackwood was chattering away, 'This is Trinity's Great Hall, not as large as ours, of course, but I believe the staircase is accounted superior to the one at Blackwood. A later addition, I have heard, to join the two wings of the house together, but I suppose you know all this, Annis, dear...'

'Are you familiar with Trinity, Miss Fallow?' asked a small voice.

'Annis? *Annis Fallow*? Good God!' called Felix, moving forward. Annis turned to him, and he saw her as unchanged in all essentials, just a little more serious than he remembered her. He took both of her hands in his. 'I did not know you were coming! It is an age. Welcome, indeed!'

'Felix! You look just the same!' she said, giving him the smile he remembered.

'I know that is *not* a compliment! Well, well, Annis Fallow!'

'Felix! You have not greeted *me*!' said Lady Blackwood with a playful sulk.

'Hello Marjorie!' he said in an offhand way that contrasted with his greeting of Miss Fallow, whom he did not look away from.

Annis gave him an admonitory look, and said, 'I also must introduce you to Miss Fleur Caldicott, Felix, who joins us on our visit.'

Lady Blackwood seethed, since it was obviously *she* who should have introduced the young lady, but part of her Grand Plan seemed to be progressing, at least. Just see how wrong Gilbert could be! Annis and Felix were getting along swimmingly.

Felix finally noticed the slender figure of a very quiet girl, standing to one side. She was wearing a sunny yellow muslin gown of a shade a little brighter than was usual in girls her age, which he judged to be about twenty. But it became her mahogany locks and her pretty face, which looked up at him with large brown eyes and a gentle look.

Marjorie had done rather better for Gaston this time. But she seemed very shy.

'Hello, Miss Caldicott, and welcome to Trinity. I am called Trinity also, Felix Trinity, and I hope that you will pass a pleasant stay here.'

'Oh,' the girl said, embarrassed and stumbling over her words, 'I … I am *sure* I will!'

He exchanged a comical look with Annis, and she linked her arm through the trembling girl's and led her forward to the salon. 'I would wager *this* salon is where they will bring us refreshments.'

'You are quite correct, Miss Annis,' said the quiet voice of the butler, opening the door.

Annis stopped. '*No!* Is that Rhodes?'

'It is miss! I am flattered that you remember me!'

'Of course I do! You helped Felix and Gilbert and I many a time when we were in a scrape.'

'I was never in a scrape,' intoned Felix.

They moved off, and found Gaston, Viscount Stanton, standing stock still on the rug before the fire, looking stiff.

'Are you Viscount Stanton?' said Annis, coming forward and holding out her hand frankly, 'you came here after I had moved away, I think, for I knew *of* you, but I do not think we ever met.'

Stanton was relieved that such a relaxed person was his visitor, and smiled his anxiety away, shaking her hand. He looked to his uncle for clarification.

'Miss Annis Fallow was a neighbour of ours, a little girl who plagued the steps of Gilbert and I for many years.'

'Oh, so your father must have owned Fallow Manor?'

'Yes,' said Annis, 'that's right, and now my cousin Chester resides there.'

Stanton must be a sensitive soul, thought Annis, for she saw him wonder if she had suffered a loss of fortune.

'My mother and I moved to a much less draughty house in Bath and were very happy there. Although, I did regret our neighbours. So, I came at your invitation because I wanted to visit some of my friends … as well as the Manor, of course.'

'This,' said Marjorie in stentorian accents, to break into Annis' taking over of the greetings, 'Is Miss Caldicott, who has accompanied us on this visit. Miss Fleur Caldicott, my nephew-in-law, Viscount Stanton.'

Miss Caldicott, who had jumped at Marjorie's commanding tone, blushed and bobbed a curtsey, miserable.

Gaston looked at her. She was very pretty, but did not seem quite aware, and was more nervous than he. Not that he was nervous, of course not. But he said gently and reassuringly, 'You are welcome to Trinity, Miss Caldicott, and I am very pleased to meet you.'

Fleur Caldicott gave Gaston's handsome face another look, then a smile, and looked more comfortable.

'Well, we shall have tea and get to know each other a little better, then the ladies and I will change for dinner. I suppose you keep country hours here still?' said Marjorie with an assumption of a frequent visitor. She was re-establishing herself as hostess and poured the tea with panache.

Annis, watching her, smiled. As they went upstairs to oversee the unpacking and to change for dinner, Marjorie said, 'Oh, Felix was just *thrilled* to see you again Annis. You can hardly have expected such a warm welcome!'

'Well, Felix and Gilbert were my friends, you know Marjorie. Childhood friends.'

'But you were so much younger! And in our Season, it was very different, after all. For Gilbert confessed to me just yesterday that he never saw you as a *woman,* you know!' Marjorie could not resist this little acid, but she was here to secure Annis' marriage, after all, so she added, 'but perhaps it was very different for Felix!'

Annis, who had been surprised to be stung by Marjorie's remark, since she thought herself past that pain, nevertheless had to laugh at this addendum. 'Not at all. Felix saw me as a sore charge of a girl whom he had had to pull from his lake time and time again.' She laughed reminiscently, 'my legs were too short to get over the stepping stones, but I kept trying so that they would not leave me behind.'

'Well, anyone can see that he admires you now, Annis!'

'Do not be foolish, Marjorie. Felix's and I share friendship, nothing else.'

'We shall see!' said Marjorie smugly. 'And Fleur, dearest, is not my nephew Stanton just as handsome as I promised?'

'He *is!*' said Miss Caldicott, 'and he has such kindness in his manner.

'Well!' said Marjorie, 'We have started aright. All things will go smoothly.'

Annis and Fleur Caldicott exchanged glances, Fleur's worried. Annis could already see a danger in Marjorie's interference. To her and Felix' simple expressions of friendship being given an insinuating commentary which might force them to treat each other differently from embarrassment, and Marjorie's crassness could also interfere with her own plan to mate the younger people. Fleur Caldicott was already terrified, Marjorie's encouragement might just make her pass out in humiliation. Annis had no opinion on matchmaking, just wished to pass a comfortable visit for all concerned. But Marjorie, she saw, could ruin it for everyone.

Could she dash off a note to her once-friend Gilbert, requesting that he send for his wife for a family emergency? Why, since she'd seen Felix, did this occur to her? She had never envisioned contacting Gilbert for anything ever again, and this kind of collusion against his wife was unthinkable. But suddenly it seemed to her that Gilbert must know who Marjorie was by now, even if he held her in great affection. Even *if?* What was she thinking? Thoughts that she had no right to. But suddenly Gilbert and Felix were her idolised older friends again, and it had seemed for the space of a thought, that he must be on their side.

She made a decision and dressed quickly, running downstairs in her yellow satin, pinning a curl up as she did so. Gaston Trinity, Viscount Stanton, was at the bottom of the stairs and watched her, laughing.

'Have you no maid to do that?' he said, but then he blushed at his own jocularity.

Annis arrived on the bottom step and answered, in the same tone as his, 'I do. And she is in my bedchamber sulking because I would not let her finish. But I wanted a word with Felix before dinner.'

The young man looked relieved at her easy manner, and said, 'You'll find him—'

'... in the bookroom, *I* know,' she moved swiftly in that direction. Then she turned back to him, her hands still up on her errant curls, and saying in her frank manner, 'Do you find me presumptuous, walking around your home with such familiarity? It is just that Trinity was something of a childhood playground of mine.'

He smiled. 'And of mine, so I understand! I hope you will make yourself at home, Miss Fallow, just as you used to. It is Felix's house of course. Stanton Park is north of here, but I have lived at Trinity for years'

'With your grumpy uncle?' She gave a giggle which made Gaston smile and skipped to the bookroom.

Felix was there as she had anticipated, but he did not look up. He heard a rustle of silk as she came forward, however, and finally lifted his head from the book. 'Annis! Pardon, I thought it was just Gaston.'

'I wanted to talk with you before dinner, Felix.'

'Delighted. Are you up to mischief?'

'No, trying to prevent some.'

'Marjorie?'

'She means to set us all to partners. You guessed of course!'

'Well, I know she has picked out poor Miss Caldicott for Gaston, but us all?'

'She told me that it was obvious how much you admired me...!'

'Good God!'

'Precisely!' She sat more comfortably on the chair she had taken opposite his. 'I thought we should talk because if either of us believe any one of her hints or suggestive remarks, all of the pleasure of this visit will be spoiled.'

'I shouldn't believe any such thing!' Felix scoffed.

'But you are looking at a spinster of thirty-six now, some would suggest that I can only be a desperate woman. Before the evening is ended Marjorie will very likely suggest that I have held a *tendre* for you since childhood.'

'Nonsense, if you had a childish *tendre* it was for Gilbert!' He gasped. 'Oh, I am sorry, Annis. I should not have said so. My tongue tends to speak my thoughts too quickly.'

'You were correct of course. Perhaps that is why Marjorie has brought me here. I have returned after all these years unmarried, and she might wish to dispose of me, in case I covet her husband.' She laughed at his small frown. 'There, I too have an ungoverned mouth.

I had no need to guard it around Mama, you see.' Trinity smiled, but there was still a line between his brows, so she added. 'You do not still think me pining for Gilbert, do you? I confess I am glad that he is not here, but that is only because ... oh, it is too hard to explain.'

'Try! I *am* interested.'

'Well, when I wished him joy, all those years ago, I think I gave myself away rather, and seeing him afterwards made me embarrassed.'

'It is very long ago. I'm sorry he hasn't come. We three could reminisce.'

'Not with Marjorie here, she may have changed, but she used to have a jealous disposition.'

'That has not changed, I think. She is even jealous of Gilbert's time spent with me.'

'Well, I am here to suggest we turn a deaf ear to Marjorie's insinuations, or else they will spoil our reunion. I hoped you would visit Chester at Fallow Manor with me, and some of the older neighbours.'

'Of course! Let us do that. It will give us an excuse to leave Marjorie behind.'

'Is that too dreadful? I do not mind her company if she didn't have the plan to match us. And who knows how she will torture the shy feelings of poor Miss Caldicott? She is a very pretty but timid child and blushes awfully when Marjorie makes a pointed remark.' She looked on, candid, 'What of the viscount? He does not look to be of a nervous disposition, but Marjorie could try the patience of a saint.'

'Perhaps I should have a word with her...!'

'You? With the unruly tongue?'

'Yours is not much better, as we have established.'

'Perhaps you could tell her that Stanton hates *hints* the most, and that he will never look at a girl who is foisted upon him.'

'She will say that it not a *foisting* but an *introduction*. She is not given to self-reflection.' He scratched his chin in a gesture she remembered. 'What if we get up before her and take off when the weather is fine? We could take a landau and drive around the county together, all four of us.'

'The children will very likely find it a bore. But we must not be selfish, but save them, too. If we go out together, they can learn a little about each other in a more relaxed way.'

'Do not let Gaston hear you call him a child! He will go because he will do anything to escape her ladyship, the little miss will go because she is biddable.' He narrowed his eyes. 'Don't tell me you are a matchmaker, too.'

'I am not. But he is handsome, and she is pretty, and stranger things have happened.' She frowned a little. 'Very well, we should go out early, and together! I'll issue the invitation to Fleur in her bedchamber this evening. But Marjorie might be deeply offended if we leave her out of things tomorrow.'

'I'll just say I know that she does not like early hours, or visiting old people who have no social function, and wished to spare her.'

'Well, we who have an evil intent, must bear the consequences, I suppose,' Annis said, practically.

Felix laughed, thinking her much braver than he remembered, and they went together into the salon to gather before dinner. 'Nice gown!' he remarked casually on the way.

'For goodness' sake, do not let Marjorie overhear you say that.'

'I've a good mind to kiss your hand in front of her to send her into transports of joy!'

'Oh Felix, it *is* good to see you again!'

'For goodness' sake, do not let Marjorie overhear you say that.'

They entered the salon, smiling at each other.

'Here comes the happy pair!' cried Lady Blackwood.

Felix and Annis exchanged a supressed laugh.

***

Marjorie's tactics over dinner were crass and self-defeating. They lay principally in forcing the men into making compliments to the ladies. *'Do you not think that Miss Caldicott's gown is of a shade that sets off her eyes this evening, Stanton?'* The viscount looked uncomfortable and said, *Just so!* in a dry tone, while poor Fleur Caldicott wanted to slip under the table. Annis reflected that she had been very much like her as a young girl, hating to attract notice. It was harder for Fleur, of course, because of her beauty.

'Dear Annis has hardly aged at all, has she Felix?' cried Marjorie over the table to Felix,

Felix merely said, 'that is what we must tell all ladies over thirty years, I believe.'

'You are over *thirty?*' had said Stanton, incredulous.

Annis was glad of the incredulity of course, since she was six years past thirty, but the unintended compliment was lessened by the tone he used for the word *thirty*. 'Yes, my lord, she said primly, 'Quite in my dotage!'

'No, no!' he began, but met her eyes. 'Oh, you are laughing at me again!'

'As if I would, viscount.'

There was much more of this kind of thing, and poor Fleur Caldicott was on her last nerve. Since the ladies chose to retire after dinner, Annis followed her to her room and asked to go in with her. As the maid took down her hair, Annis said, 'You must not mind Lady Blackwood. She means well, you know. The viscount knows her and attributes all his embarrassment of this evening to her and not you, Miss Caldicott, so do not fear.'

'Oh, I know she is being kind, but I feel as though the poor viscount is being pressured to … well,' she ended.

'I know *just* what you mean. She is doing the same thing to Felix and me, who are only old friends who wish to remain comfortable with each other. I spoke with him of it tonight, fearing that Marjorie's broad hints might make one or other of us self-conscious. We are determined not to do so, and so we have conceived of a scheme where we four go out early together on our own, doing things that Marjorie does not care for, you know, and have a more relaxed day, and only come home for dinner.'

'Oh, should we?' said Fleur displaying hope. 'Is it not insufferably rude?'

'Well, not of *you*, Miss Caldicott. You are just accepting my invitation to meet my friends. We could probably take your maid, too, in case we separate for any reason, though I do not think we shall.'

***

The bright morning that was displayed from the breakfast room window promised clement weather for their expedition. As expected, Marjorie did not make an early breakfast, so leaving word with Rhodes the butler proved an easy escape. Felix ordered the landau rather than a closed carriage.

'Very optimistic!' approved Annis.

'I'll drive, Dobbs!' he told the coach man and leapt onto the box.

Annis was about to join him when she looked at the faces of the younger two, suddenly strangely oppressed. Enforced proximity of young persons who were not previously acquainted was awkward indeed, so she suggested, 'Fleur, why do you not climb up with Felix? He is an unpleasant individual, but he will not bite.'

Fleur looked relieved, as did the young viscount, who handed Annis into the carriage like a gentleman. Felix had merely held out his hand

and yanked at poor Miss Caldicott, but it made her giggle, and she sat on the box beside him, smiling over her shoulder at Annis.

'You are a great card!' Gaston said, and then. 'Oh, I beg your pardon, Miss Fallow, I should not have said...'

'Call me Annis, for Felix will. It will allow me to wander around your house freely, since it suggests intimacy.'

'Well, I am honoured. And you must call me Gaston, of course.'

'It is a noble name!'

'An old family one, I believe.'

'Oh yes, there is a portrait of the third Viscount in the upper gallery, is there not? He looked formidable!'

'As am I,' said Gaston, 'you shall see it, if Marjorie wants to play more tricks.' He pulled a face with lowered brows for a glower.

'Oh, I can see the ancestral resemblance!' cried Annis. He pulled the face again, to hear her laugh, and she said, 'Oh, stop, stop! You are much too handsome to mar your features that way!'

Gaston blushed. 'Am I handsome?' he asked.

She laughed at him, 'You must know you are! You must be told so all the time.'

'Only by such people as Marjorie, or matchmaking mamas. But you do not care for such things so I can ask you ...am I?'

She was touched, but a little conscious now herself, though that was absurd, she merely laughed and said, 'Extremely!'

'Thank you.'

'You are welcome.'

'And I, who am not given to bestowing compliments much, am therefore free to tell you...'

'Because I do not seek to be a viscountess?'

'Yes. So, I can tell you, in case you have not heard it recently, that you are one of the loveliest creatures I have ever seen.'

For the first time in at least ten years, Annis blushed to her ears.

'What is he saying?' said Felix from the front seat.

'That Miss Fallow is lovely,' Fleur Caldicott informed him.

'Well, that's true. You have improved with age, my dear!'

'Don't let Marjorie hear you say so.'

They all laughed. They had reached the Manor, and as they drove into the gates, Annis said, 'Well, viscount, if you have anything remotely pleasant to say to Miss Caldicott, you should do so now, for you must guard your tongue over dinner.'

'Miss Fallow, Annis...!' pleaded Fleur.

'No, she is quite correct. I think you such a pleasant girl, Miss Caldicott. And pretty, also,' said Gaston, simply.

'I'm glad that is out of the way,' said Felix. 'And you are right on both counts.'

Fleur looked warmed by this.

'You are too sensible to take Gaston's words to heart, Miss Caldicott,' remarked Felix. 'He will probably be unpleasant to you over dinner, only to stop Marjorie in her tracks.'

'It is not efficacious. She will redouble her efforts,' said Annis from the back seat.

'I am glad she did not hear the viscount call me pretty, I should have been *crushed by* embarrassment then!' said Fleur Caldicott.

Felix looked down at her, amused. 'But you are not now?'

'No, for he said so after he had called Annis *the loveliest creature he has ever seen*, so his compliment to me shall not go to my head.'

'*That* is what you said?' asked Felix, over his shoulder, before stopping the carriage, 'you shall not flirt with my friend, scamp!'

'Do not be silly, Felix. He was being kind to an old maid,' laughed Annis.

They got out of the carriage. Annis's cousin Chester greeted her with warmth and welcomed the visitors inside.

A very pleasant visit ensued, after which the escapees from Trinity had a lingering luncheon at the inn. The day was fine, and even Felix smiled once or twice. Fleur was much more relaxed, and the conversation flowed.

Annis, assured that the young people had lost their initial shyness and fear of consequences, attempted a Marjorie move to have Fleur sit in the back with Gaston, but the girl had mounted the block beside Felix before she had a chance. They were talking about books, Annis realised, and this was the one topic Felix might hold forth on for a month. But it was evident that Fleur was holding her end of the conversation.

'What are they speaking of?' said Gaston with a lifted eyebrow at Annis.

'Natural philosophy, I believe!'

'Oh! Very interesting, I am certain,' he said politely. There was a beat, and they both guffawed.

Back at Trinity, they were faced with the disapproving face of Lady Blackwood. However, Annis, before dinner, was able to tell Marjorie how *well* her Grand Plan was continuing, 'For the children are very friendly after our day together.'

'It seems even Felix smiled once,' Marjorie remarked, feelings somewhat ameliorated.

'Indeed!'

'You and he getting along?'

'Oh, famously!' said Annis, without a lie. All this because she did not want to hurt Marjorie any more than necessary and leading her to misunderstand a little might make for a more peaceful visit.

After breakfast the next day, Annis lost Fleur and finally found her with Felix in the bookroom, silently reading. They seemed peaceful together there, so Annis did not disturb them.

She went for a walk, and Gaston caught up with her.

'Should you not have a maid with you?'

'At Trinity? It seems absurd. And I am past the age of needing a constant chaperone.'

'No woman who looks as you do is past that age.'

Annis turned to him, stopping for a moment, a trifle cross. 'Am I to be your *practise,* Viscount Stanton?'

'Practise?' said Gaston, confused.

'A safe woman to practise the art of flirting with, so that you can later woo young ladies with more finesse.' She was evidently a little put out, and continued walking.

He sighed, keeping in step. 'My title does the wooing for me, I find.'

She looked soothed a little. 'Young cynic,' she quipped.

'Yes.' He said after a moment. Then after another pause, he added, quite seriously, But today I speak so because I have met the woman of my dreams.'

'Gaston!' Her tone showed shock and a scold at once.

'Annis!' he laughed. He looked, she thought, unfairly and unbearably handsome, staring at her. Confident too, and she frowned at his evident happiness. When she did not reply, he finally looked unsure, but hopeful still, 'You said yesterday that you hadn't laughed so much in an age. Is that not since you met *me?*'

She strode ahead, almost running, and when he caught her on a wooded path, he grasped her arm.

'It is absurd!' she said. 'I am twelve years your senior!'

'I am used to living with old people.' He quipped. 'Only think of Felix!'

She laughed again, tears in her eyes. 'I must not, for *your* sake my dearest boy.'

'We have met only for a day, and I am your dearest boy already, as you are my love already.' Then he looked down more seriously, 'In a little moment I will be your dearest *man*, not boy,' he warned her, then clasped her to him, kissing her passionately.

Annis succumbed for three wonderful minutes in his arms, then pulled away, saying, *'Oh!'* and picked up her skirts, running to the house. She could not see Marjorie, not now, so she ran to her friend Felix.

'Oh Felix, something *dreadful* has happened.' She began but was stopped by a sight she had not expected. Felix Trinity was standing with Miss Caldicott suspended in his arms, and Fleur was blushing rosily.

The viscount had just caught up and looked on, closing the door whose knob was still in the hand of Annis, he took the opportunity, dog that he was, to caress it.

'Miss Caldicott turned her ankle, and I just caught her...!' began Felix in a confused tone.

Fleur hid her head in his shoulder, her blush getting deeper.

'And kissed her, I'll be bound!' said Gaston heartily.

'Oh...!' said Miss Caldicott's small voice, and Annis noticed that Felix held her closer and had not made a move to set her free.

'*Felix!*' said Annis shocked.

Trinity met her eye, '*What* dreadful thing occurred.' He asked, reminding her of her entrance.

'Oh, I just asked Annis to marry me,' the viscount said blithely.

'You *did?*' asked Annis turning to him.

'Of course I did, silly. Why else would I have kissed you?'

'Oh, Felix,' pleaded Annis, looking at him, 'is it too awful? I am too old for him?'

'I think it splendid!' said a little voice from Felix's coat.

'Do you, my love?' Trinity asked, looking down at her.

'Oh, Felix!' said Fleur, at being so addressed. 'I mean Mr Trinity.'

'Felix!' said Annis, pleading for his attention.

'I don't know! I am too old and dull for this lovely creature, but I won't let anyone else have her!'

'Oh....!' Said Fleur, her head burrowing more deeply into him.

'But I am female. The succession.'

'Children can never be depended on to arrive or not arrive. Happiness, my old friend, comes rarely. You must not miss it this time, my dear!'

Anni turned to the viscount. 'But when you are fifty, I will be sixty-two, Gaston!'

Felix said, as helpful in his way, 'And you will have lost interest him by that time and be happy when he flirts with other ladies in town.'

'I never will!' protested Gaston.

'I see your warning, Felix,' said Annis, nodding, Then determinedly, 'I should be open to the possibility. Well, I will be.'

'Don't be absurd!' cried Gaston, taking her hand again. 'Felix, I'll kill you!'

Somehow Gaston's hand had slid around Annis's waist again, and she looked towards him, '*Can* I be so selfish Gaston? Can I say yes?'

'Darling!' an interlude occurred that made Felix turn his back with his burden and deposit her on the sofa opposite the fire. He joined her there, and Gaston, finishing his kiss, opened the book room door and called for the butler/

'Some champagne, I think, Rhodes'

'At this hour, my lord?' said the old butler, not disobedient, but shocked.

'The occasion calls for it,' Gaston put his hand about Annis's waist once more and the butler bowed low.

The four sat in shell-shocked silence for some time, until the champagne was served.

Fleur was trembling, and Felix handed the glass to her, 'Have some of this against the shock, darling!'

'It is a shock!' she said. 'Has it really happened?'

Annis looked at her. 'I think it has.'

'Are you sure, Felix, that you want...?' began Fleur.

'I did not think I wished for a wife. But I find I am very wrong.'

Gaston laughed. 'And I thought I'd have to settle on someone for the sake of my name.'

'And I was perfectly happy living alone.'

'You'll be happier living with me,' said Gaston, smugly.

'Well,' said Felix, sardonic again, 'Which of us will tell Marjorie that her Grand Plan has worked already ... just not in the way she thought it would?'

An exchanged look and an explosive laugh, and then Fleur, with more wit than Annis had given her credit for, said she would put their three names in a hat so that they might choose.

'Why three?' enquired Gaston.

'Because someone must hold the hat!' she said innocently.

Felix Trinity put one finger under her chin and turned her to him. 'I was drawn to you because you could sit silently with me. But now I think you might be a minx!'

'Have you changed your mind, then, Felix?' asked Annis gaily.

'No,' he sighed resignedly, 'I am blinded by love, as the poets say.' He looked over at his childhood friend, with Gaston seated on the arm of her chair, his arm over the chair back. 'And you, my dear?'

But it was Gaston who replied, taking up Annis's hand and kissing it. 'I won't let her change. Never in this life.'

'You've grown up since yesterday,' Trinity remarked.

But Gaston was locked in his true love's eyes.

'Felix! Do you know where Marjor—' Lord Gilbert Blackwell broke off, seeing strange sights, First Felix Trinity, with his arm around a *female*, drinking champagne, then Annis Fallow looking even lovelier than he remembered her, seated with Gaston on the side of her chair, his arm draped over the back, also drinking champagne. Indeed, they all were. 'What's this?' he said, stopped in his tracks.

'Wish me happy, Gilbert!' Annis smiled up at him.

'Annis!' he stepped forward and she went to meet him, grasping his hands. This time it was Blackwood who was betrayed by his voice, 'I do, Annis, I do!' But his tone trembled.

He looked over at the viscount, standing nearby. Gaston had not been concerned at first, since it was only *Gilbert* after all, but something in their intensity made him walk forward to her shoulder.

'Oh Gilbert,' Annis was saying sincerely, looking at Blackwood with tears in her eyes, 'We can be *friends* again.'

'What a *good* thing,' he said, moved, 'I have missed you.'

Blackwood's eye moved over to Gaston, who now seemed anxious. Annis gave her old friend a wry look, wondering about his opinion on their differences, but Gilbert only said, to the viscount, 'You lucky young dog! Treasure her.'

'I will, Gilbert.'

Felix had lifted his woman from the sofa again, into his arms, 'Do not struggle,' he ordered, 'be good

'But I only need the support of your arm...!' Fleur protested.

'Nonsense! Your foot must rest during dinner and then we'll see.' He gave her a stone-faced look, 'Did I ask you to wed?' he asked her.

'Not yet!' said Fleur's shy voice, but amused.

'Well, what do you think?'

'Yes. I think yes.' she said, quiet but firm.

'That's settled then,' said Felix, walking to the door.

'How did this happen? said Blackwood barring his friend's way.

'She fell over, I caught her up and it seemed I must kiss her.'

Blackwood's eyebrows rose, while Fleur hid in Felix's coat.

'You're not more surprised than I am,' sighed Felix. 'Knew I liked her from the first, but didn't expect ... but there it is.'

Blackwood gave way, shaking his head for comic effect, as Marjorie came in, 'Felix have you seen Blackwood? Rhodes tells me he has—' she gasped. 'What is *happening* here?' she said looking at her young charge in Felix Trinity's arms.

He walked past her, 'Hurt her ankle,' he said briefly as he passed.

Gaston took Annis's hand, kissed it in a grand gesture, and put it through his arm and walked past also. 'Dinner will be soon, my lady!' he smiled at her agape mouth.

'*Annis!*' Then Marjorie looked at her husband, shocked. '*Gilbert!*'

'Gaston would never have wed any of your simpering ladies, I told you so. He's as stubborn as Felix.'

'But not *Annis*...! And *Felix*...! What *will* I say to Miss Caldicott's mama ...?'

'Didn't think much of your Grand Plan, my dear,' said Blackwood laconically, turning her in the direction of the dining room, 'but it appears to have borne fruit!'

He strolled off for dinner, his distraught wife at his heels.

Chapter Eleven

Esther and the Impulsive Proposal

'Good evening, sir,' said a breathy, shaking voice of a female, with a hint of determination, 'I have come to tell you that you are the most handsome, wonderful man I have ever seen, and I wish to suggest a candidate for your future wife. In short, myself.'

The girl was before him, and her hand he now held in greeting, an intimacy he had granted automatically when she had thrust it towards him with nervous determination.

Viscount Vigo Destry had been just about to go to the card room after a desultory look around the provincial Assembly Room, wondering how long he had to stay here this evening. Grandmama was not so ill as she had claimed, and he was here with her and two aunts who wished to find him a bride '*from a pot you have not stirred as yet*' his grandmother had said.

He would return to London tomorrow, but tonight he would dance with one or two of the girls that he was required to and calm the choppy waters of familial disapproval. Obviously, since his brother had died, it now behoved him to become a sensible man and marry. But grief, plus a natural predilection to be free, made this, assuredly, not the time.

Tony Loxburgh, his cousin who resided here in Harrogate, was by his side — Destry's only respite from boredom this evening.

Two young women had approached, one purposefully, one catching up to match her stride, and they were as dull as the other young ladies here, he feared. They must be, he thought, friends of Tony's. But the female with the round face and truly awful gown in a sickly green shade, had thrust a hand out at him in a determined fashion. He took it so as not to be impolite to this child who did not know how to behave. She had even features, which seemed designed not to draw attention, with exception of a dent in one spherical cheek — a permanent dimple. Despite it, she did not look flirtatious or *coming*, just serious and animated by some fearful mix of happiness and dread.

'Good evening, Miss ... eh, I must assume you are a friend of Loxburgh's.' He spoke because the handshake had gone on a beat too long, her fingers rather a claw about his, and the introduction might be over quicker this way. 'Is this your jest, Tony?' he looked to his cousin who seemed shocked and amused both.

'No,' the girl said before his cousin could answer, 'I do not know your name, or this gentleman's, sir, but I felt moved to say those words to you when first I saw you. Perhaps if I repeat it again, we might both believe it.'

He raised his brows, trying to sound bored, 'Aunt Harriet or Aunt Sally?' he enquired.

'I beg your pardon?'

'Which sent you — was it Lady Huxley, or Mrs Driscoll, or perhaps my grandmama, Countess Knox?'

'I am acquainted with none of those ladies. I simply came because … you took my breath away.'

Destry had looked to Tony, who was brim-full of hilarity and surprise, and who gave him an amused shrug. Destry pulled the hand that she had captured away from her abruptly.

'I cannot return the compliment, madam,' he said, a trifle coldly.

Her lids dropped over her eyes, and she sighed, but answered stoically, 'You have your own freedom.' It was unlikely that you would favour me, of course.'

'I might be married or betrothed,'

'I did not think of it.' Then she put her head to one side, looking at him gravely, 'But even now, I do not think you *are*.' She blushed as confusion overcame her again, and said, 'But you should know, at least, that you are someone's dream.'

'I daresay my cousin is *many* young lady's dream, miss,' said Tony between amusement and a scold, 'but they do not approach him in a ballroom and tell him so.'

The round face turned to Loxburgh for a fleeting moment with a candid look that dropped his jaw. 'No? But I found I must.' She turned again to Destry. 'Being rejected by you, sir, is a greater honour than being accepted by any other. I have held your hand,' she took the hand that had grasped his in her other and held it out to him, as though for his regard, and continued in the same sentence, 'I shall not marry another in this life.'

'Are you abducting me?' Destry said, still in shock, as she began to turn away.

'I beg your pardon?' she answered, stopping, seeming genuinely confused.

'Is this not a form of moral kidnap? You threaten me with your spinsterhood? I do not think much of your admiration if you seek to *wound* the man you admire.'

She turned back to him fully.

'Oh, I see,' she nodded seriously. 'Yes, I *quite* see your point.' Then she looked elated and put a hand to her cheek, which flushed anew, 'But *look* how well I have chosen! Only a decent man would give a fig for the marriage prospects of a young lady who had so rudely approached him at a ball.' She smiled at him, the dimple deepening and more appearing at the corners of her mouth, her hand to a swelling chest. 'You are everything I thought you and *more*!' Then her practical tone recurred, and she nodded again as though in assent. 'Very well, I *shall* marry, and soon. Mr Cruikshanks has approached my Papa, I believe. Perhaps I should marry him.'

She gestured across the ballroom, and it might be supposed that it was to a square bodied fellow considerably older than Destry, for the man was looking at them fixedly from halfway down the ballroom.

'He must be twenty years your senior!' remarked Destry.

'Oh, no, I am twenty-six years, you know. And he is quite the first man to wish to marry me. I should suppose him no more than thirteen years my senior.'

'You *cannot* be twenty-six years.'

She smiled very briefly. 'My whole family looks like babies. It is the chubby faces. Papa could pass for twenty-five, you know.'

Destry was annoyed at the diversion, and his tone came out as chiding, rather than the cold detachment he wished for. 'In any case, do not be so ridiculous as to wed, or stay unwed, only for a sudden silly notion of liking a stranger in a ballroom.'

'You mistake me,' she said, as calmly as she could. 'I do not *like* you; I *love* you.'

He gasped, outraged. Her eyes, neither the brightest or prettiest he had seen, were a complicated colour of browns and greens and held his own with a naked look, which, like her ridiculous words, he could not respond to. So, he said coldly, and in the most ungentlemanly manner he had ever used to a lady, 'Why do I speak to you? Go now!' He hoped it would be enough to shock her from her ridiculous dream.

She blushed, had the sudden face of a young girl who knew that she had humiliated herself, but she pulled herself together to say calmly, 'Very well. Farewell, sir, and I wish you a happy life indeed.'

She left, her shocked and embarrassed friend trailing behind her muttering nervous words in her ears, and now Tony Loxburgh was closer to Destry and laughing heartily.

'What on earth was that? Extraordinary female! Let us play cards, old fellow, to relieve your temper.'

'Yes,' he followed his cousin but looked over his shoulder. The female was headed to the square gentleman, in as straight a line as the crowded ballroom would permit.

'Hold!' he called out her. The ballroom occupants in the vicinity looked on amazed at the raised voice, as a young woman in an unbecoming gown turned in answer to the summons of the most talked about young man in the room.

'Vigo, what are you about, man?' said Tony in a low, repressive voice.

Destry answered in a lowered tone himself. 'She will very likely become betrothed to that dolt in the first sentence she says to him, the idiot child.'

'What has that to do with you?' said Tony, pulling on his elbow discreetly. 'And how do you know the fellow is a dolt?'

The young woman in the dreadful gown had turned and was standing still, twenty feet from him, looking at him directly, as her friend pulled at her elbow, rather less discreetly than Tony Loxburgh's yank at his cousin Destry.

Destry crooked a finger and the girl weaved through the dancers to come back. 'Because I can just tell he is by looking at him,' he hissed in answer to his cousin, as the young woman made her way.

'Like your admirer can tell you are *the best man in the world*?' jeered Tony Loxburgh in his ear.

The woman was facing Destry again, but at a safer distance.

'Do not become betrothed,' he ordered her, staring into her brown and green and grey eyes, 'or mention the word betrothal, for at least a month. During that time, think carefully about the rest of your life. Think how it could be useful, and indeed, joyful. There is more than one person who might make one happy, I believe.'

She had been paying rapt attention, holding his eyes in the way he had found unnerving from the first, but at the last she shook her head at him, 'For some people, perhaps.'

'One can make one's own happiness.'

'You adjure me *not* to marry, then?' she asked, looking at him gravely.

'Of course not. I adjure you to *think* a little. I adjure you to wait until your head and your heart are both ready.'

'My heart is full and ready this evening. I told you so. I do not think marriage has much to do with one's head.'

'You are much mistaken. One should judge the character of one's intended closely, one should judge what life is acceptable and right to go on harmoniously together. If a spouse were to irritate one every day for the rest of one's life, it is likely to make the other person very unhappy also. For some other partner, the irritant you experience might *not* be so annoying, do you see? And your irritating spouse might have gone on to find contentment with *someone else* instead of feeling your disappointment daily, even if you do not voice it.'

'You know of such a relationship.' She said — and it was a statement. He paled, but she continued, 'I see. Even if one knows one will never love again, one must choose a harmonious partner.'

'Yes,' It was Destry's turn to nod gravely. 'And besides, how can you know you can never love again? I once found a dog in the street. It smelt dreadful for months and chewed everything in the house and bit the servants, and yet eventually I loved it dearly — indeed, more than my other dogs.'

'Do not tell me any more lovely stories about yourself, or my heart will break with longing.' She said it breathily, but in a scolding tone, that returned again to the practical. 'But what you mean to say is, one might come to love *anything*.'

'I suppose,' he said, aware that this strange person was concentrating on his every word in a way he was not at all used to, being a fairly frivolous fellow. It occurred to him also that this admission suggested he could come to love the round-faced child in the dreadful gown, too. But her reply surprised him.

'Then wouldn't Mr Cruikshanks do?'

He was annoyed but could not think why. 'That is not what I meant. I mean, I suppose he *might* do, but do not adopt the dog before you are sure you might like it.'

'*You* did!'

'But I would not do so for a *wife*. A lifetime's companion.'

'Ah!' she gave him a shining look, as though she were touched anew. 'Many men think of a wife as *less* of a companion than a dog, I believe. Your view of married life seems so much gentler. *A lifetime's companion* is your description.' She did the thing of looking her admiration again, and it seemed different in quality than the admiration he had been shown before by young ladies. Shy admiration, flirtatious admiration, disguised admiration that played hard-to-get. Hers was a rawer variety, almost mad in its intensity. But her voice was gentle as she asked, 'What kind of wife would you like?'

This was dangerous ground where he would not permit the zealot to step, so his reply was coldly dismissive. 'I do not think about it. I do not wish to be married as yet.'

The woman sighed. 'Men are free to think so, of course. Women may not.'

'I do not see why.'

'Are you the eldest of your family?'

'Yes.'

'You look so. The rightful heir to something or other,' she sighed. 'I too, am the eldest, but my much younger brother will inherit. He does not like me, and so ...'

'Your future feels unsafe,' he finished for her.

'Will your father make no provisions?' asked Tony at his side.

She flicked a glance at him. 'Those he can. If he remembers to.'

'You think he will not.' Destry said, but it was a statement, not a question.

She pulled herself up a little taller, it seemed, though she was still below average height. 'My father is heedless, and somewhat wild. He is just the sort of man who will be knocked over, when in his cups, by a carriage. And he will have meant to make his will another day.'

'I see,' said Destry, aware that this conversation was being marked by many now. People wondering what his connection to the girl was, since this had gone on longer than mere civility. It was well to finish it. 'Perhaps you should marry Mr Cruikshanks after all.'

'Yes,' she answered, irritating him again.

'But take a month before you mention it again. Or allow him to. Think about what things you might want or need.'

'I have only ever wanted one thing.'

'Me?' he laughed harshly. 'Well, you cannot have me. Did you think your purposeful plan would work?'

'I walked to you within ten seconds of seeing you. I just needed to put my vision before you.'

'It did not attract me. It merely made me wish to send for a physician.'

Her eyes looked a question, but then she nodded her understanding, 'They should incarcerate the insane. I see.' She nodded again in acceptance.

The way she always agreed was unnerving. Time to finish this completely.

'Goodnight Miss, eh…'

'Good evening, sir.'

'Might I have your name?'

She paused then asked, 'Is it important? We shall not see each other again.'

'No,' he agreed coolly.

'It was quite wonderful knowing you.' She gave a sad, tremulous smile.

'You know nothing about me.'

'Every word you have spoken to me, every moment we have spent together gives lie to that. I thought I knew you from across the room. And it has been borne out.'

'Ridiculous.'

'Is it? Your concern for me. For my rashness. For my future. What other man would care?'

'When one meets an insane person, one should try to prevent them from harming themselves or others. That is all it is.'

'Oh, do not mistake me, I was not suggesting you were showing me more concern than you might to *anyone*, but am only noting that your character is splendid. The very fact that your concern is universal puts you on a par with gods. I am not disappointed in you.'

'Not disappointed? I as good as told a young lady she was not well-favoured. That hardly qualifies as splendid.'

'Well, what were you to do other when a complete stranger tells you she will be your future wife? *Naturally* you had to restrain her forcibly so that she would have no hope at all.' Her look was compassionate, and it pierced him. 'I expect that impolite remark cost you dearly. I am sorry to have forced you to make it, though it was not at all unjust or untrue. My mother told me as a child that it was not necessary to say everything that I thought out loud. And that indeed I *must* not. So, I understand that I forced it upon you, and that it must have cost you to be impolite, even if you were true to your impression of me.'

He looked over her head, trying to seem as remote as ever, but he was shaken.

'I shall take your advice and secure my future.' She seemed to see the flicker on his face and said, in what he thought, enraged, might be a consoling tone, 'But not before a month has passed. I promised you.'

He looked back at her, a hint of anger in him at her presumption that he would care, but she had turned to join her small pale friend who was still on the outskirts of their group, and they melted into the ballroom, but not in the direction of Mr Cruikshanks at least.

He ambled with Tony to the card room, an arm on his shoulder in a friendly fashion, but his cousin felt him tremble a little.

***

Somehow, though her dress was plainer than many ladies around her, Viscount Destry saw the girl in the buff-coloured gown almost at once. It was at a draper's merchant in London, where he had accompanied his mama and sister Ellen in choosing muslins to refresh their wardrobes, since they were now in the middle of the Season.

'Isn't that...?' Cousin Tony said at his side.

Ellen leant across, 'Do you know someone?'

'That little girl in the beige gown and hat...!'

'Quiet!' hissed Destry, incensed.

Ellen's eyes were alight with mischief, 'Yes? How do you both know her?'

'She came flat up to Vigo at a Harrogate assembly and introduced herself as his future wife.'

'She?' said Ellen, taking in the unremarkable female in the simple gown and bonnet, 'She doesn't look either shameless or pert.'

'Who does not?' said Lady Destry, their fashionable mama, overhearing.

'Vigo's *future wife*, Mama.' And so saying, Ellen walked briskly over to the girl, who was with an older woman, respectably, but unremarkably, dressed in a grey velvet pelisse.

Destry turned to his cousin. 'I will *kill* you!' and followed. As his mother, craning her neck with an open mouth was about to follow, he said. 'Stay here with Tony, Mama. Ellen is jesting.'

Ellen, having reached her target, had introduced herself in a shameless way. He saw that the girl and her companion looked bemused.

'Excuse me ladies, I wonder if I might make myself known to you?' At the elder lady's confused nod, she continued. 'I am Lady Ellen Destry ... and then seeing a blank look from both added, 'I believe you,' here she smiled at the younger of the two, 'are acquainted with my brother — Viscount Destry, you know.'

The round-faced girl with the dent of a dimple in one cheek looked confused, 'I do not believe...' and Destry thought, coming forward, *did she really not know my name?* But then she saw him behind his sister, and said, 'Oh, it is *you*!' in the breathy tone he knew.

Her elder companion had begun to introduce herself, 'I am Mrs Dalton, and this, I suppose you know, is my niece Miss Esther Dalton, who makes a short visit to town from Harrogate.'

'We are fortunate then, to have met you,' said Ellen. 'Are we not, Destry?'

'Indeed,' he said in a congested tone.

Miss Dalton's eyes were not particularly large, but he remembered the perfect intensity of her look. It seemed she could not speak and she held a hand to her chest, over her plain brown Spencer.

This was perfectly dreadful. He ought not to have followed Ellen on her quest for mischief. To approach a woman who had declared her love for you, and whom you had rejected, was insanity. And cruel.

'You are choosing muslins for the Season for Miss Dalton?' his dreadful sister continued brightly.

'Not today,' said the aunt, after a pause when her niece did not answer. 'Today we choose for a trousseau.'

Ellen's face fell, it seemed her mischief was spoilt, but despite himself Destry was calculating. 'It is but three weeks...' he muttered.

'Oh,' said the young girl with a flush, 'it is not for *me*.'

'My daughter Charlotte is to wed Captain James Cooper,' said Mrs Dalton with cheer. 'Are you perchance, acquainted with the captain?'

'I am afraid not, ma'am,' said Ellen sadly, 'but a wedding is always a great thing.' She smiled at the lady and said, 'I wonder if I could borrow your niece for a moment. I should like to introduce her to my mother.'

Destry took his sister's elbow and nipped it. 'No need to interrupt your important endeavour, ladies. My sister has too much time on her hands.' He turned and smiled at Ellen, a deadly look in his eyes, 'Let us go back, my dear, mother awaits us.' His eyes drifted to Miss Dalton, who was still looking on in utter amazement, but with an evident thrill that he found awful to note. She may have brought everything upon herself, but something in her raw regard made him not wish to wound her more than by his rejection. 'Miss Dalton, I apologise.' This last was said in a low voice and with a grim nod.

He kept the grip on Ellen's arm as she said a polite goodbye. He used it to drive her to their mama and Tony, a perfectly grisly look upon his face.

'Let us go ... *now!*' He hissed as they rejoined his mother and cousin.

His family followed as they left the establishment, and Destry kept his dark silence as he called for the landau. Tony Loxburgh tried to escape, misliking the look in Destry's eye, and Ellen was losing her earlier bravado. 'I said nothing...' she began.

'Stow it!' rasped Destry crassly, and Ellen stood gazing a little fearfully at her Mama, who raised her eyebrows at her daughter and mouthed *What?*

Once in the landau, into which Destry also thrust a reluctant Loxburgh, his mama began, 'What has made you so angry, Vigo? I saw at once when looking at the girl that Ellen had *jested* about *your future wife* ... but what *is* the jest, and why should you now be so angry?'

'Because my imbecile cousin and more imbecilic sister have just caused real damage ... oh, I cannot begin to explain to you.'

'I was only remarking...!' started Loxburgh — and then '...and *I* did not go to the girl,' he added like a schoolboy shifting the blame.

Ellen gave him a dark look, then defended herself, 'Well, if she really was so *coming* as to introduce herself to you as *your future wife*, I do not see how what I have done is worse...'

'She *did?*' cried his mother, 'That little girl? She did not look the sort.'

'She is not the sort,' Destry said.

'Oh, then Tony *lied* as usual,' sighed Ellen, 'I suppose he will claim it is only *funning*...'

'She did say so,' Loxbugh protested, 'I *heard* her!'

'Well, that is beyond everything ...' said his mama, shocked. 'What kind of forwardness ... ambition...?'

'*Stop!*' said Destry in a commanding voice he did not use to his mother, 'She *did* say so to me, but she did not say so to be pert. She is not ambitious, I think, for she did not even know my name.'

'So *you* believe...!' said Tony, cynically.

'No,' Ellen said suddenly and consideringly, 'Vigo is quite right. She had no idea who *I* was, either.'

'But why would a girl go and *say* such a thing to a gentleman...?' said Lady Destry, still shocked.

'She is not a girl ...' Destry said in passing, 'she is twenty-six years old.'

'Ah, a desperate spinster, then,' said Ellen, with sarcasm.

'No! She said it was ... the impulse of the moment.'

'Ah! A *coup de foudre!*' said his mother, understanding. 'Well, you are very handsome, my dear boy. But still, her behaviour is beyond the pale.'

'No more than Ellen's,' said Destry coldly. 'I cannot remember when I have been more furious with you.'

'Does her own behaviour not deserve a riposte?' replied his sister. 'And I was very respectful, only introducing myself as a sister of a friend, and Mrs Dalton said they were there to buy muslins for a trousseau, then Vigo came up and muttered something about it *only being three weeks ...*'

'What did that mean dear?' asked his mother.

'*I* know,' said Loxburgh informatively, 'He told me afterwards the little miss had determined that since she could not have my handsome cousin, she would not marry. And when Destry told her not to be an idiot, she agreed to marry a man who had already offered for her.' Then he paused, leaning forward insinuatingly, 'but Destry recommended to her that she should wait a month and consider it carefully, instead of being impelled by that night's events.'

'You spoke to her a good deal, my dear,' said his mother frowning.

'She was ... I cannot well explain it,' said the viscount musing, 'But she is a lady I *rejected*, and one that I *approached* today.'

'Oh yes,' agreed his mama, 'you had much better have stayed away from her my dear. She might have *hope* and only think how *dreadful...*!'

'*Precisely*, but since my sister fancied a jest at my expense, I have now committed a sin against the young lady.'

'You might have sent Tony after Ellen.' His mama said.

'I feared her tongue, and Tony is useless in delicate situations, as today's events only show!'

'I *still* don't think it is *my* fault,' said Loxburgh, 'If Ellen hadn't taken me up so ...!'

'Well,' said Ellen, 'I admit I was impulsive, but I do not see how much worse I am than *she*... Miss Dalton's words to you were *much* more shocking than my impromptu introduction.'

'But your interjection *drew me to her*. A person I already wounded and would not hurt again for the world. And the difference between

Miss Dalton's words and *yours* is that hers were utterly brave and sincere, while yours were a crude and cruel jest.'

There was a silence. His sister and cousin looked shamefaced. Finally, his mother said, 'She said more,' she guessed, 'than that she was your future wife. She made a *confession of affection* for you.'

He did not answer, looking grim.

'And you do not doubt her. Not a bit.' His mother concluded.

'Well, many women feel affection for Vigo and his fortune of course,' said Tony, trying to lighten the situation.

'But she did not *know* of his fortune,' said Ellen, wondering.

'I imagine she might have guessed it from the work of his tailor,' said Tony.

'But Vigo does not believe so. *He* thinks she is utterly brave and sincere,' continued his mother.

Everyone looked to him, with interrogating eyes.

'Well, I do not say so easily,' he admitted, 'but only that, however much I fear she may be mistaken in her sudden interest in me, however little I deserve it, however far from returning her regard I may be, I think that I know her to be *truthful*.'

'How long did you speak to her?'

'A few minutes only.'

'And yet you know so much...' his mother said.

'I have to think of a way to stop this,' Destry said, grave again. He called to the driver.

***

He went back to Oxford Street, back to the draper's establishment, and found that the Dalton ladies had not left. It was truly time consuming to buy a trousseau, apparently.

He approached them and bowed briefly. 'Mrs Dalton ... might I now take your niece on a drive around the park? I shall take her back smartly.'

There was no maid, but a drive in an open carriage was supportable, so Mrs Dalton was all smiles when she agreed. 'I shall see you presently, my dear Esther.'

'Yes aunt.' Miss Dalton replied in a quiet voice. She was shocked again, but there was no help for it.

Destry handed her up to the box of the landau, after getting rid of the groom who had driven it for his family, and joined her, taking the reins himself. She, sat trembling beside him.

'Miss Dalton, I must apologise for today.'

'You have no need to, but it is like you to do so.'

'Do not speak as though you know me,' he said annoyed, 'it is disquieting.' This was not how he had wished to start his conversation.

'I beg your pardon. You apologise for what...?'

'For approaching you today ...'

'Ah! You are worried you gave me hope. Do not fear, I was moved for but a moment. I saw at once that your cousin must have repeated something to your sister, and she must therefore come to see the Bedlamite,' this was said in an amused tone, but he detected some humiliation. She continued, 'I was just so taken aback that I could not say so and spare you this meeting. Go to Fredericks Street, if you please. It is my aunt's house.'

'We have not been away long enough,' he said in a cool tone.

'I beg your pardon?'

'For you to say that an old friend asked to be remembered to your papa and took you on a drive to tell you so.'

'I do not lie well.'

'I know,' he remarked, briefly.

She looked down at this, grasping her reticule and smiling furtively.

'What do you smile at?'

'It is only ... you talk rather as if you know *me*, Viscount Destry.'

'You tease me...'

'I shouldn't. But it also amused me that you remembered the duration of our pact.'

Again, despite his wish to be distant, he could not help but ask, 'You have considered?

'Yes. I cannot marry Mr Cruikshanks, for he does indeed annoy me.'

He asked, despite himself, 'In what manner?'

'He speaks constantly of the *cost* of everything. Not in guineas, but by *comparison. I fear my carriage is less expensive that Mr Smith's and my silver watch chain finer than Mr Brown's ...*' she said in a deeper voice. 'I should certainly come to show my ... annoyance after a year or two, if he continued.'

'You mean your *contempt*, not annoyance.'

'Do I?' she smiled. 'What a *deal* you seem to know of me.'

'I have lost my bearings,' he said dryly, changing the subject. 'Which direction is Fredericks Street?

She indicated and they spent the rest of the drive in silence. When he pulled up at her door, he said, 'I appear to have been rude again. Goodbye, Miss Dalton. I wish you everything you wish for yourself.'

'Do you?' Her grave face seemed to laugh once more. 'You really should *not*, you know. For your own protection.'

'I...!'

'Goodbye, my lord. Do not fear, I doubt we shall meet again.'

'Yes...' he said shamefaced.

'Do not look so ...' she said, in a comforting tone, 'you have done me no new hurt. And the first hurt was my own fault entirely. But...'

'Yes?' he asked, looking at her.

'I wish we had not met again,' she said, sadly.

***

Though he looked, he did not see her at Almacks. He knew it was unlikely that a mere Miss Dalton should be given vouchers in any case. Her aunt was a respectable matron by her looks, but hardly of the Beau Monde. He had looked, of course, only so as to *avoid* her. He wished to give neither of them the humiliation of being in the same company again.

It was two weeks before he saw her once more, at a large rout given by the Enderbys, the fashionable young duke and duchess. It seemed that everyone in London was here, and he saw her near one of the impromptu dance floors that were scattered about the house and garden: at one, a chamber ensemble played minuets, and at another, far enough away so as to only hear the chamber music distantly, were some rustics playing country dances, then also a Germanic-looking group, playing waltzes and quadrilles in a large room overlooking the garden. He wondered briefly what connection she might have to be invited here, but the Enderbys were not at all stiff-rumped, and he had friends in many walks of life.

Miss Dalton was beside the country dancing party in the garden with her aunt and another lady. A gentleman, vaguely known to Destry, bowed and evidently requested her to dance, and the viscount had the sudden thought that his moratorium on betrothal had ended last week. The man she danced with now was, he remembered, one Sir Nigel Atwell, a prosperous widower of around forty. He watched as she danced with gusto. The country dances suited her simplicity, he thought. He doubted she would comport herself elegantly in the quadrille or waltz. Did she waltz? He must suppose so, for she had told him that she was six and twenty.

Rather than melting into another room, where a variety of casual entertainments had been arranged: some tumblers in one corner of the garden, a quiet, ill-lit room in the house where poets and other writers read their work, or a lady sang, he pushed himself through the light crowd of people watching the dancers, right to the edge of the dance floor to get a better view. She smiled a good deal as the widower addressed some remarks to her, and he saw that there were even more available dimples. Another deep one in the opposite cheek, some pretty dents just at the side of her lips, too. She looked absurdly youthful, dancing with much enthusiasm and less consciousness than the ladies around her. Her dress tonight, though plain, suited her. It was a pale green silk, a colour that seemed reflected in her eyes. Then she saw him.

She stumbled a little, then the dimples disappeared, but for the permanent one that helped her look less than her age. She gazed off at once, and her steps became tamer, stiffer. What was he doing standing so visibly? He backed into the crowd, standing on a lady's dropped fan in the process, asking for her name and address so that he might replace it.

He watched Miss Dalton leave the dance floor and enter the house, with her female friends and relatives, Atwell did not follow, but was now dancing with another.

'Destry! Miss Burton enquired about you.' Tony said. 'What do you look at?' then he grasped Destry's arm suddenly. '*Attention*, Lady Ferguson approaches on the left side, with two daughters in tow. We are not safe here.'

Destry heard it all, but he was counting garden doors, taking note of the one the Dalton party used to enter the ducal abode. He moved off, Tony following on his coattails, 'Dashed rude of me if the Ferguson woman knows that I had spotted her! She will complain to m'mother!'

The viscount merely continued on his way. She was not in the first room, where a supper table was surrounded by ravenous guests making up plates for themselves and carrying them off in the vague hope of finding a seat somewhere else. He weaved through a cloakroom and a room where an Italian contralto sang to an interested crowd, before he found her in the room where the chamber music played. He stood well back then, but after a while he noted that her left shoulder seemed to turn a little as he moved around the back wall, and her rear view remained to him, as though her shoulder was the boom that moved her sails, always away from him.

It was, he thought, only because in a whole rout of female personages there was one, she, whom he was not permitted to dance with, that he therefore *wished* to dance with her. She was asked again, someone introduced to her, and she smiled briefly and agreed.

Tony was rattling on, and had evidently not seen her, for no witticisms on the subject of *future wife* left his lips. He said, 'Miss Burton is over there with that pretty friend of hers, Miss Lively. Never was a girl so well named!'

This pierced through Destry's consciousness, he looked to Miss Burton, whom he had hoped to see tonight, and was appalled at the notion of joining the dancers. What if Miss Dalton were to see? It would be to slap her face. He could not do it.

He left the room abruptly and did not see his mother approach the party with the girl in the green silk.

***

Destry did not dance with Miss Burton or anyone else, for he left the duke's rout at the unfashionably early hour of eleven thirty.

He only drove and went to the races or clubs in the next few days. He kept away from the more fashionable parks when driving, and did so only on his own, taking up no passengers

In bed at night, he tossed and turned, remembering the boom that was her shoulder, which he became convinced was the proof that even when she could not *see* him, her awareness was mystically still tuned to his presence, and to avoiding it. There was a smattering of freckles on the muscle that led from neck to shoulder, he remembered, and they were pretty.

There had been ten days of this, ten days of being called to order when he did not hear his family's words addressed to him, and so his mother took his hand and sat him beside her on a small gilt sofa, nodding away her family and the footmen.

That night he attended small ball on the edge of the fashionable district which marked the public betrothal of Captain Cooper to Miss Charlotte Dalton. His mother, his sister, and Tony all entered too, although only his mother knew why they were there.

***

An incident then occurred that led to a shocked room.

After it, two family parties stood opposite each other, with the pair of interest, a man and a woman, having only two feet between them.

Tears seemed to spring from Esther Dalton's eyes and flowed in a river down her cheeks. It was, thought the onlookers, a fair response to the incident.

Destry stood trembling before her, and a smile, a bouquet of dimples, had lit up her face and she trembled, too.

It seemed the room held its breath until the voice of Miss Dalton's newly betrothed cousin Charlotte said, in a clear tone. 'My cousin is unwell, Lord Destry. Might you take her to the garden ...' and here she gestured to another door adjacent, '... for some air?'

This was a rather shocking suggestion, but in light of the *incident* it seemed applicable to the viewers, even if it spoiled the chance to overlook the spectacle somewhat.

'Ah, yes!' the viscount said and pulled Miss Dalton's hand through his arm, almost destroying the nosegay she held. The girl tripped after him as he led her away.

When they reached the adjoining room, where the garden doors were situated, he pulled her into his arms.

'Oh Destry, Destry!' she sobbed against his chest.

'Esther!' he said wrapping her more firmly in his arms, 'Don't cry, don't cry, my love.'

'I never *dreamed*...!'

Destry pulled away a little, tipping up her chin so that she looked at him, and smiled, 'Yes you did! Within ten seconds of seeing me.'

'Oh yes, I *did*,' she smiled through her tears. 'But afterwards...'

'I have thought of nothing but you since that night in Harrogate. Every word you said to me, your ridiculously elevated view of my character...'

'No...!' she protested.

'Yes. But Mama has told me, after meeting you and seeing my feelings for you, she said that I can spend my life living up to it, even if I am unworthy now.'

'The lady that spoke so kindly to me that evening at the rout, of nothing at all and yet I felt her *attention*, was that your mother?' he nodded, and she continued, responding to his remarks, 'But unworthy?' she shook her head. 'It is *I* ...! I am aware, *newly* aware since I came to London, what manner of society you hail from. The world would think it is *I* who am not worthy.' The serious eyes that he loved so well looked back at him.

He laughed at her. 'But *you* do not.'

'No. The world sees the difference in our fortune and appearance. It is all true,' this was said in her reasoned serious tone, but it changed as she added passionately, 'but they do not know, they can never know, how much I *love* you.'

'No,' he agreed, smiling, 'Only *I* know. I was humbled by it, but I found I *trusted* in it completely. It was my mama who made me see it.' His hand cupped her face looking down at her, taking her in. 'You are so lovely.'

It was her turn to laugh at him. 'You did not think so at first...'

He sighed, pinching her cheek with one hand and pulling her closer with the other.

'No. I am a shallow man.' He confessed, 'And to be fair, you ought never to wear that dreadful gown again.' She wrinkled her nose, frowning, and he laughed at her but said, in a tender voice, 'But every feature, every freckle and dimple on your skin is beloved by me now, I assure you.' And now his eyes were serious, too, as he pulled away to let her see his expression when he said, 'Your staggering devotion I should never find again. Your honest spirit is unmatched in this world. I know it.'

Her breast swelled and she breathed up at him, *'Destry!'*

'May I kiss you, my darling?'

She was shy, but almost swooning into him already. Her reply was as honest and open as he had come to expect from her, 'I am yours — you may do what you will with me.'

It still surprised him into a bark of laughter. He hugged her tight, smiling, 'Do not say so to a man in love!' He pulled back a little, giving her a little bow, 'I shall woo you royally, my lady.'

She came towards him, back into his arms, and said into his coat, 'No need for wooing...'

He kissed her soundly, making her ready tears spring up again.

'What a watering pot you are,' he said, wiping the tears with his thumbs, and laughing at her to lighten the mood. He pulled her back to him and held her again as though his life depended on it. 'Darling, we must go back, or your reputation will be in tatters.'

She, too, clung to him. 'I do not care for...!' she began passionately.

'But *I* do!' he chided, to make her smile again. 'You must think of *my* name, you know, for it will soon be your own, my sweetness.'

'Oh Destry!!' She gasped again, putting her head on his chest and clutching at his coat as though he might run off. She laughed a little to herself, in an attempt to calm down. 'My moment of insanity has come to this.'

One hand grasped her curls, bringing her nearer again. 'Your moment of clarity, of *brave honesty* has come to this, and I shall never be able to thank you enough in this lifetime. I might,' he said with a shudder, 'have missed my own soul.'

They stood so for a minute, before he kissed her trembling cheek and pulled her hand through his arm again.

'Mind the flowers!' she giggled. 'I shall want to press them tonight as a keepsake.'

'We shall keep them in our family bible, my love.'

It was too much for her again, the tears almost fell, but he shook the hand he had captured, and she stiffened her spine, nodding to him as he looked down to see if she had herself in hand.

They came out of the library to the compliments of friends and family; she did not leave his arm the evening long.

On the carriage ride home, his family regarded his smiling face. He grinned, 'Is it normal, Mama, that I miss her already?'

Since they were only half a street from her, his mother shook her head and said sadly, 'You are *desperately* in love, are you not, my dear boy?'

He looked out on the city streets, lit by flickering lamps and the occasional torch and silently agreed. 'Esther!' he thought, 'My Esther!'

The inciting incident earlier had been this:

That evening, his family had been a trifle late in arriving to the engagement party that his mother had managed to procure an invitation for. There were perhaps fifty guests here already, the hosts stood before the fireplace of the largest salon the house boasted.

Viscount Destry, dressed formally in knee breeches, a well-cut coat and with a diamond pin in his high muslin cravat, weaved his way through the company to *her* family party, his elegant figure capturing the attention of the crowd as he did so. He was the most arresting and elevated person in the company.

He must suppose that it was the captain (whatever his name was) and his betrothed at the centre of the host party, looking well dressed and happy, and flanked by the aunt and the likely uncle. On one side of them Miss Esther Dalton stood, in the green silk again, probably her best evening dress. The viscount's own party, of mother, sister and cousin, followed him, a little to his rear. He was mildly aware of them and that someone in the crowd of guests had greeted him, but he continued on his path.

Miss Dalton jerked as she saw the viscount approach and their eyes met. She tried to drop her lids, but the sheer power of his will, he believed, meant that she could not. Their eyes held. No one else was aware of his destination, perhaps, until he stood before her, eyes still fixed. He produced a nosegay of violets and held it out, she reached for it, but her eyes were still on his and she was in a daze, so he had to place it in her gloved hand, glancing down for a second to accomplish it. He looked up again and held her eyes. There were no greetings to the hosts, no sideways glances at all.

A hush had fallen around the room.

'Viscount...' began the aunt feebly. But the young betrothed girl, who was Miss Dalton's cousin, Destry supposed, had held the mother back.

'Miss Dalton,' the viscount had said, in a carrying voice. 'I have come to tell you that you are the most beautiful, wonderful woman I have ever seen, and I wish to suggest a candidate for your future husband. In short, myself.'

This is the incident that had caused both Miss Dalton's streaming tears and her joyous smile, and her response made Destry fall anew.

This is what held the room aghast as they looked on — even his own family, shocked at his wording, and his heightened tone of public declaration. But Tony grinned. Destry had given the girl's own words back to her precisely, and looking at Miss Dalton's shining face, Loxburgh suddenly saw how lovely she was, and true. Destry's tone was, thought Loxburgh, perhaps a *public* apology for the girl's previous *private* humiliation.

He looked to Cousin Ellen and his aunt, Lady Destry. The incident had moved them all, both the viscount's words and the girl's response. It was a job well done.

Also By Alicia Cameron

Regency Romance

Angelique and Other Stories: https://mybook.to/Angelstories
Angelique was named by her French grandmother, but now lives as Ann, ignored by her aristocratic relations. Can she find the courage to pursue her Destiny, reluctantly aided by her suave cousin Ferdinand? With lots of added stories, including: **Ann and the Cinderella Gown, and Abigail and the Lost Years, Anabel and the Impudent Smile, Amelia and the Bad Betrothal**

Beth and the Mistaken Identity: getbook.at/Beth
Beth has been cast off as lady's maid to the pert young Sophy Ludgate, but is mistaken as a lady herself by a handsome marquis and his princess sister. Desperate to save the coach fare to London, she goes along with them, but they do not let her escape so easily.

Clarissa and the Poor Relations: getbook.at/Clarissa
Clarissa Thorne and her three friends have to leave their cosy School for Young Ladies after the death of Clarissa's mama. all must be sent off as poor relations to their families. However, Clarissa suddenly inherits Ashcroft Manor, and persuades the ladies to make a bid for freedom. But can she escape their unpleasant families? The Earl of Grandiston might help.

Delphine and the Dangerous Arrangement: getbook.at/Delphine
Delphine Delacroix was brought up by her mother alone, a cold and unloving childhood. With her mother dead, she has become the richest young lady in England, and is taken under the wing of her three aunts, Not quite trusting them, Delphine enters a dangerous arrangement with the handsome Viscount Gascoigne - but will this lead to her downfall?

The Fentons Series (Regency)

Honoria and the Family Obligation, The Fentons 1 https://getbook.at/Honoria
Honoria Fenton has been informed that the famous Mr Allison is to come to her home. His purpose? To woo her. She cannot recall what he looks like, since he made her nervous when they met in Town. Her sister Serena is amused, but when Allison arrives, it seems that a mistake might cost all three there happiness.

Felicity and the Damaged Reputation, The Fentons 2
https://getbook.at/Felicity

On her way to London to take a post as governess, Felicity Oldfield is intercepted by Viscount Durant, who asks her to impersonate his cousin for an hour. When, in an unexpected turn of events, Felicity is able to enjoy a London Season, this encounter damages her reputation.

Euphemia and the Unexpected Enchantment, The Fentons 3
https://getbook.at/Euphemia

Euphemia, plain and near forty, is on her way to live with her dear friend Felicity and her husband when she is diverted to the home of Baron Balfour, a bear of a man as huge and loud as Euphemia is small and quiet. Everything in her timid life begins to change.

Ianthe and the Fighting Foxes: The Fentons 4 https://getbook.at/Ianthe

The Fighting Foxes, Lord Edward, his half-brother Curtis and Lady Fox, his stepmother, are awaiting the arrival from France of a poor relation, Miss Ianthe Eames. But when Ianthe turns up, nothing could be further from their idea of a supplicant. Richly dressed and in high good humour, Ianthe takes the Foxes by storm.

The Sisters of Castle Fortune Series (Regency)

Georgette and the Unrequited Love: Sisters of Castle Fortune 1
https://getbook.at/Georgette

Georgette Fortune, one of ten sisters, lives as a spinster in Castle Fortune. She refused all offers during her London Seasons, since she fell in love, at first glance with the dashing Lord Onslow. He hardly knew she existed, however, but now he has arrived at the castle for a house party, and Georgette is fearful of exposing her feelings. She tries to avoid him, but Onslow treats her as a friend, making Georgette's pain worse, even as he makes her laugh.

Jocasta and the Cruelty of Kindness: Sisters of Castle Fortune 2

https://getbook.at/Jocasta

At a house party in Castle Fortune, Jocasta's beau had fallen for her sister, Portia. Now Jocasta is back in London and has to suffer the pity of the friends and family that care for her. Only Sir Damon Regis treats her without pity, and she is strangely drawn to him because of it.

Katerina and the Reclusive Earl: Sisters of Castle Fortune 3

https://getbook.at/Katerina

Katerina Fortune has only one desire, to avoid going on her London Season altogether. On the journey, she hears of a recluse, who dislikes people as much as she. Katerina escapes her father and drives to offer a convenient marriage to the earl, who refuses. But an accident necessitates her stay at his home, and they discover they have more in common than either could have believed.

Leonora and the Lion's Venture: Sisters of Castle Fortune 4

https://getbook.at/Leonora

The pretty Fortune twins come to Town, and Leonora has only one object in view: The Honourable Linton Carswell. But Foggy Carswell is too craven to be caught – he is not a marrying man. While trying to save her twin Marguerite from the results of her own romantic naivety, Leonora has her work set for her. But a number of family alliances begin to aid the unlikely pairing.

Marguerite and the Duke in Disguise: Sisters of Castle Fortune 5 https://mybook.to/Marguerite

Marguerite Fortune, bereft of her newly married twin Leonora, is heading back to her Castle Fortune home with only her two unsympathetic male relatives for company. At an inn she meets another Leo, this time a man mountain, who saves her from harm. When her father diverts their journey and abandons Marguerite to make a match at Dysart manor, Leo arrives too. They are soon embroiled in awful plots, kidnap and even murder.

Naomi and the Purloined Journal: The Wild Marchmonts #1: mybook.to/Naomi

The Marchmonts, including the Earl and Countess of Tremaine, live at Tremaine Towers, but the two Marchmont sisters, Ophelia and Queenie, and brother Charles find it strange when the earl permits another ragbag family of Marchmonts, distant cousins, to come and make their home. The earl's family call them the Wilds and mistake them for poor relations, but nothing could be further from the truth. Some truth is revealed in Naomi's journal, which is read by another brother of the earl, Eliot. He is amused and drawn to the writer.

Ursilla and the Baron's Revenge: The Fentons Book 5

Edwardian Inspirational Romance
(typewriters, bicycles, and leg-of-mutton sleeves!)

Francine and the Art of Transformation: getbook.at/FrancineT
Francine is fired as a lady's maid, but she is a woman who has planned for every eventuality. Meeting Miss Philpott, a timid, unemployed governess, Francine transforms her into the Fascinating Mathilde and

offers her another, self directed life. Together, they help countless other women get control over their lives.

Francine and the Winter's Gift: getbook.at/FrancineW
Francine and Mathilde continue to save young girls from dreadful marriages, while seeing to their own romances. In Francine, Sir Hugo Portas, government minister, meets a woman he could never have imagined. Will society's rules stop their union, or can Francine even accept the shackles of being in a relationship?

Chapter Twelve

A Sample Chapter of Honoria and the Family Obligation: The Fentons Book 1

Blue Slippers

'He has arrived!' said Serena, kneeling on the window seat of their bedchamber. She made a pretty picture there with her sprigged muslin dress foaming around her and one silk-stockinged foot still on the floor, but her sister Honoria was too frozen with fear to notice.

'Oh, no,' said Honoria, moving forward in a dull fashion to join her. Her elder brother Benedict had been sitting with one leg draped negligently over the arm of the only comfortable chair in the room and now rose languidly to join his younger sisters. After the season in London, Dickie had begun to ape the manners of Beau Brummel and his cronies, polite, but slightly bored with the world. At one and twenty, it seemed a trifle contrived, even allowing that his long limbs and handsome face put many a town beau to shame.

Serena's dark eyes danced wickedly, 'Here comes the conquest of your triumphant season, your soon-to-be-fiancé.'

Dickie grinned, rather more like their childhood companion, 'Your knight in shining armour. If *only* you could remember him.'

'It isn't funny.'

Serena laughed and turned back to the window as she heard the door of the carriage open and the steps let down by Timothy, the one and only footman that Fenton Manor could boast.

'Oh, how did it happen?' Honoria said for the fifteenth time that morning.

Someone in the crowd had said, 'Mr Allison is approaching. But he never dances!' In confusion, she had looked around, and saw the throng around her grow still and part as her hostess approached with a tall gentleman. With all eyes turned to her she stiffened in every sinew. She remembered the voice of Lady Carlisle introducing Mr Allison as a desirable partner, she remembered her mother thrusting her forward as she was frozen with timidity. She remembered his hand lead her to her first waltz of the season. She had turned to her mother for protection as his hand snaked around her waist and had seen that matron grip her hands together and glow with pride. This was Lady Fenton's shining moment, if not her daughter's. Word had it that Mr Allison had danced only thrice this season, each time with his married friends. Lost in the whirl of the dance, she had answered his remarks with single syllables, looking no higher than his chin. A dimpled chin, strong, she remembered vaguely. And though she had previously seen Mr. Allison at a distance, the very rich and therefore very interesting Mr Allison, with an estate grander than many a nobleman, she could not remember more than that he was held to be handsome. (As she told Serena this later, her sister remarked that rich men were very often held to be handsome, strangely related to the size of their purse.)

There was the waltz; there had been a visit to her father in the London house; her mother had informed her of Mr Allison's wishes and that she was to receive his addresses the next afternoon. He certainly visited the next afternoon, and Honoria had been suffered to serve him his tea and her hand had shaken so much that she had kept her eyes on the cup for the rest of the time. He had not proposed, which her mother thought of as a pity, but here she had been saved by Papa, who had thought that Mr Allison should visit them in the country where his daughter and he might be more at their leisure to know each other. 'For she is a little shy with new company and I should wish her perfectly comfortable before she receives your addresses,' Sir Ranalph had told him, as Honoria's mama had explained.

Serena, when told, had thought it a wonderful joke. To be practically engaged to someone you could not remember! She laughed because she trusted to good-natured Papa to save Honoria from the match if it should prove unwanted; her sister had only to say "no".

'*Why on earth do you make such a tragedian of yourself, Orry,*' *had said Serena once Honoria had poured her story out,* '*After poor Henrietta Madeley's sad marriage, Papa has always said that to marry with such parental compulsion is scandalously cruel.*'

And Honoria had mopped up her tears and felt a good deal better, buoyed by Serena's strength of mind. To be sure, there was the embarrassment to be endured of giving disappointment, but she resolved to do it if Mr Allison's aura of grandeur continued to terrify her.

'And then,' her sister had continued merrily, 'the rich Mr Allison may just turn out to be as handsome as his purse and as good natured as Papa — and you will fall head over heels with him after all.'

The morning after, Honoria had gone for a walk before breakfast, in much better spirits. As she came up the steps to re-enter by the breakfast room, she carelessly caught her new French muslin (fifteen and sixpence the yard, Mama had told her) on the roses that grew on a column. If she took her time and did not pull, she may be able to rescue herself without damage to the dress. She could hear Mama and Papa chatting and gave it no mind until Mama's voice became serious.

'My dear Ranalph, will you not tell me?'

'Shall there be muffins this morning, my dear?' said Papa cheerfully.

'You did not finish your mutton last night and you are falsely cheerful this morning. Tell me, my love.'

'You should apply for a position at Bow Street, my dear. Nothing escapes you.' She heard the sound of an embrace.

'Diversionary tactics, sir, are futile.'

Honoria knew she should not be privy to this, but she was still detaching her dress, thorn by thorn. It was incumbent on her to make a noise, so that they might know she was there, but as she decided to do so, she was frozen by Papa's next words.

'Mr Allison's visit will resolve all, I'm sure.'

Honoria closed her mouth, automatically continuing to silently pluck her dress from the rose bush, anxious to be away.

'Resolve what, dearest?' Honoria could picture her mama on Papa's knee.

'Well, there have been extra expenses – from the Brighton property.' Honoria knew that this was where her uncle Wilbert lived, her father's younger brother. (Dickie had explained that he was a friend of the Prince Regent, which sounded so well to the girls, but Dickie had shaken

his head loftily. 'You girls know nothing. Unless you are as rich as a Maharajah, it's ruinous to be part of that set.')

Her father continued, 'Now, now. All is well. If things do not take with Mr Allison, we shall just have to cut our cloth a little, Madame.' He breathed. 'But, Cynthia, I'm afraid another London Season is not to be thought of.'

Honoria felt instant guilt. Her own season had been at a rather later age than that of her more prosperous friends, and she had not been able to understand why Serena and she could not have had it together, for they borrowed each other's clothes all the time. Serena's intrepid spirit would have buoyed hers too and made her laugh, and would have surely helped with her crippling timidity. But when she had seen how many dresses had been required — one day alone she had changed from morning gown to carriage dress to luncheon half dress, then riding habit and finally evening dress. And with so many of the same people at balls, one could not make do - Mama had insisted on twenty evening gowns as the bare minimum. However doughty with a needle the sisters might be, this was beyond their scope, and London dressmakers did not come cheap. Two such wardrobes were not to be paid for by the estate's income in one year. Honoria had accidentally seen the milliner's bill for her season and shuddered to think of it — her bonnets alone had been ruinously expensive. She had looked forward to her second season, where her wardrobe could be adapted at very little cost to give it a new look and Serena would also have her fill of new walking dresses and riding habits, bonnets and stockings. If she were in London with her sister, she might actually enjoy it.

'Poor Serena. What are her chances of a suitable match in this restricted neighbourhood?' Mama continued, 'And indeed, Honoria, if she does not like this match. Though how she could fail to like a charming, handsome man like Mr Allison is beyond me,' she finished.

'Do not forget rich,' teased her husband.

'When I think of the girls who tried to catch him all season! And then he came to us – specifically asked to be presented to her as a partner for the waltz, as dear Lady Carlisle informed me later — but she showed no triumph at all. And now, she will not give an opinion. She is strangely reticent about the subject.'

'Well, well, it is no doubt her shyness. She will be more relaxed when she sees Allison among the family.'

'So much rests upon it.' There was a pause. 'Dickie's commission?'

He laughed, but it sounded sour from her always cheerful Papa. 'Wilbert has promised to buy it from his next win at Faro.'

'Hah!' said Mama bitterly.

Honoria was free. She went towards the breakfast room rather noisily. 'Are there muffins?' she asked gaily.

'How on earth do you come to be engaged to *him*?'

Honoria was jolted back to the present by Serena's outcry. She gazed in dread over her sister's dark curls and saw a sober figure in a black coat and dull breaches, with a wide-brimmed, antediluvian hat walking towards the house. She gave an involuntary giggle.

'Oh, that is only Mr Scribster, his friend.'

'*He* you remember!' laughed Serena. 'Is he as dull as his hat?' Honoria spotted another man exiting the chaise, this one in biscuit coloured breaches above shiny white-topped Hessian boots. His travelling coat almost swept the ground, and Serena said, 'Well, he's more the thing at any rate. Pity we cannot see his face. You should be prepared. However, he *walks* like a handsome man.' She giggled, 'Or at all events, a rich one.'

The door behind them had opened. 'Serena, you will guard your tongue,' said their mama. Lady Fenton, also known as Lady Cynthia (as she was the daughter of a peer) was the pattern card from which her beautiful daughters were formed. A dark-haired, plump, but stylish matron who looked as good as one could, she said of herself, when one had borne seven bouncing babies. Now she smiled, though, and Honoria felt another bar in her cage. How could she dash her mother's hopes? 'Straighten your dresses, girls, and come downstairs.'

Benedict winked and walked off with his parent.

There were no looking glasses in their bedroom, so as not to foster vanity. But as they straightened the ribbons of the new dresses Mama had thought appropriate to the occasion, they acted as each other's glass and pulled at hair ribbons and curls as need be. The Misses Fenton looked as close to twins as sisters separated by two years could, dark curls and dark slanted eyes and lips that curled at the corners to give them the appearance of a smile even in repose. Their brother Benedict said they resembled a couple of cats, but then he would say that. Serena had told him to watch his tongue or they might scratch.

The children, Norman, Edward, Cedric and Angelica, were not to be admitted to the drawing room — but they bowled out of the nursery to watch the sisters descend the stairs in state. As Serena tripped on a cricket ball, she looked back and stuck her tongue out at the grinning eight-year-old Cedric. Edward, ten, cuffed his younger brother and threw him into the nursery by the scruff of his neck. The eldest, Norman, twelve, a beefy chap, lifted little three-year-old Angelica who showed a disposition to follow her sisters. On the matter of unruly behaviour today, Mama had them all warned.

As the stairs turned on the landing, the sisters realised there was no one in the large square hall to see their dignified descent, so Serena tripped down excitedly, whilst her sister made the slow march of a hearse follower. As Serena gestured her down, Honoria knew that her sister's excitement came from a lack of society in their neighbourhood. She herself had enjoyed a London season, whilst Serena had never been further than Harrogate. She was down at last and they walked to the door of the salon, where she shot her hand out to delay Serena. She took a breath and squared her shoulders. Oh well, this time she should at least see what he looked like.

Two gentlemen stood by the fire with their backs to the door, conversing with Papa and Dickie. As the door opened, they turned and Honoria was focused on the square-shouldered gentleman, whose height rivalled Benedict's and quite dwarfed her sturdy papa. His face was nearly in view, Sir Ranalph was saying, 'These are my precious jewels!' The face was visible for only a moment before Serena gave a yelp of surprise and moved forward a pace. Honoria turned to her.

'But it's you!' Serena cried.

Everyone looked confused and a little shocked, not least Serena who grasped her hands in front of her and regarded the carpet. There seemed to be no doubt that she had addressed Mr Allison.

Honoria could see him now, the dimpled chin and strong jaw she remembered, and topped by a classical nose, deep set hazel eyes and the hairstyle of a Roman Emperor. Admirable, she supposed, but with a smile dying on his lips, he had turned from relaxed guest to stuffed animal, with only his eyes moving between one sister and another. His gaze fell, and he said the most peculiar thing.

'Blue slippers.'

To read on:
getbook.at/Honoria

Chapter Thirteen

A Sample Chapter of Georgette and the Unrequited Love: The Sisters of Castle Fortune 1

If you were to see all the Fortune sisters together in a line, you would be living in a fairy tale, for the girls, first because their mama was a trifle frail, and later because she was no longer with them, were too unruly ever to have been held in line for more than a second without some of them escaping to another room in the cavernous Castle Fortune, or into the rivers and wilderness beyond. For the benefit of this presentation, we will imagine them all kept in place to shake your hand. We shall capture them all in this day of 1813, and make it a sunny day. First will be Miss Fortune as was, the lovely and gentle Violetta, twenty-three, who must now disappear into the mist of Scotland to be with her husband. Loud and vibrant Cassie, twenty-two, is next, but her equally loud swain, Mr Hudson, has swept them off to Somerset, where the whole neighbourhood may hear their business from a mile away. Next there is Georgette, twenty-one, who is the principal subject of this tale. She has particularly large eyes, and has now become Miss Fortune in her turn, being the eldest unwed sister. Mary, twenty, her romantic and wilful sister, ran off with a Mr Fredericks, a music master, and they made their poor home in Bath. If Mr Fredericks hoped that marriage to the daughter of a Castle might increase his wealth, he was disabused of this notion after he met his father-in-law, Baron Fortune. Susan, eighteen, the plainest of the girls (which is to say not plain at all), married sober Mr Steeplethorpe, and seemed quietly content at her bargain.

So, our reception line now has only the unmarried Fortune ladies. Georgette now lives with the shame (her neighbours said) of having two younger siblings marry before her. Next is the sprite Jocasta, at seventeen not too like a fairy of the tales in behaviour, but who nevertheless entranced London this season with her wispy gaiety. The final four girls are not out yet and have seen little beyond the castle grounds and their few friends in the district. Red-haired Katerina, at sixteen, still thinks boys are boorish and stupid, an opinion no doubt suggested by her closest male acquaintance, her brother George (at twenty-five the only male sibling and proud heir to his father's dignities and debt). Portia, at 15, was rather more romantic, with hair a shade between the blond of Jocasta's and the brunette of Georgette's. She is taller than her sisters. The little twins, at 14, were probably the prettiest of the bunch (which is to say very pretty indeed), with still-white blond curls and big blue eyes. They would arrest the eye together in a ballroom in another three or four years.

Georgette, the median age of all her married sisters, was now on the shelf, doomed to haunt the shades of Fortune Castle till her death, unless her brother George were to eject her on the day of his inheritance. If George remembered the days of her childhood when Georgette had still seen the point of poking a bully in the eyes, perhaps he would do so, and swiftly, too. But most probably, he would let her stay to keep up the numbers of people he could ignore, insult and command.

Chapter 1

She was invisible, Georgette discovered. Quite invisible. She had suspected as much in the glazed-over glances the other guests to this house party had cast over her during the introductions, but this longed-for but entirely unexpected meeting with the Marquis of Onslow had completely underscored the matter. He had even reached past her to shake her father's hand and had touched her arm in passing, raising her heartbeat until it seemed the organ would leave her chest, without any seeming awareness of having done so.

One *could* blame Papa perhaps, but with ten daughters and one son (heaven be praised) to provide for, and no wife living to aid Lord Fortune with understanding the subtleties of female feelings, she did not really think that she could. She had quite understood that she, the third daughter of the impoverished baron, had to surrender her place in the London season to allow her younger sisters their turn at society. Their eldest sister, twenty-three-year-old Violetta (named for their dead mother) was already wed to her Scottish gentleman before Georgette had come out. Georgette had enjoyed two seasons already, one with elder sister Cassie, who had married the eligible, if very loud,

Mr Hudson. This slight defect that Georgette had discerned in his otherwise excellent, convivial character was shared by Cassie herself, who talked as though addressing a congregation even at breakfast, and who had been used to clattering downstairs in satin slippers as though the blacksmith had shod her. After Cassie's baby was born last year, Georgette had visited her home in distant Somerset and had informed her father afterwards that the child's lungs seemed to have double the capacity of each parent, making him audible ten miles hence. Her father had remarked that he would write to his daughter, kindly understanding that such a journey as the three days it would take to reach Castle Fortune should on no account be undertaken with an infant, and that they could henceforth meet during the London season for his beloved daughter's convenience. How thoughtful.

Georgette's second season had been with her younger sister Mary, who married (much to her father's wrath) a mere Mr Fredericks, who had been employed to teach them the pianoforte. Both sisters could play, but not exceptionally, and their father had conceived the notion that it was young ladies of musical talent who snared the richest, that is the most eligible, of gentlemen — an opinion he came to rue. Mrs Fredericks now lived in genteel poverty with her swain in Bath and seemed happy enough, thought Georgette, but where they might dispose of future children in two rooms was beyond her. Perhaps they might be suspended in tiny hammocks on the ceiling, she'd considered as she'd regarded the linen slung on the washing pulley in their tiny kitchen, but what to do with them on laundry day exceeded her imagination.

Susan, 18, had wed a quiet country gentleman much in her own style. This had occurred in the previous season, when Georgette remained at home to make way for Jocasta Fortune, her pretty blond seventeen-year-old sister, who had already shown herself popular in town, so she had heard.

With three of her sisters wed already after Georgette's second season, her father's looks toward her had suggested that she had rather let him down. The cost of each season was a prodigious run on the estate every year, and some decent settlements from an eligible *parti* might have eased a situation which, with six daughters still to provide for, seemed never-ending. After her last season, two years ago now, when they had returned to the crumbling Castle Fortune, he had looked at her from beneath his bushy eyebrows. 'You are not bad looking,' he barked, as though contemplating inwardly, 'even if your bosom suggests you might run to fat at a later date.' Georgette had swallowed with difficulty. 'But young men don't think of that. You don't have much conversation of course, but your birth is good and you have a small portion from your mama, which makes you at least respectable. All those gowns and bonnets,' he lamented, 'and *no one* could be persuaded to take you!' He shook his head and tutted.

When Susan got married the next year, he could not look at Georgette for a week without audibly betraying his great disappointment. 'Still here, miss? Eating my meat when even your younger sisters—' he shook his giant head with the shaggy mane of hair and muttered into his soup, 'Females! What use are females at all — especially unwed females? A leech for life, I suppose.'

There had been two people prepared to take her, who had indeed offered for her, had her papa but known, and others whose interest Georgette had, with difficulty, discouraged. The first offer was from a deliciously conceited, round-bodied clergyman, bound for a bishopric, he told her confidentially during only the first dance. It was in the family, it transpired, that all the second sons became bishops (though his grand-uncle had disappointed his family by rising no further than Dean). Georgette had accepted his offers to dance as was polite, but Cassie had been unable to understand why she allowed the fusty cleric to walk her to the supper room, or take her apart to sit and talk a dance away. The sad truth was that Georgette, though listening with a grave air to the Reverend Mr Fullerton's conversation, had been inwardly bursting with delight. He was so utterly ridiculous that she found herself fuelling his climb to the precipice of bumptious absurdity. The dreadful propensity of hers to judge the ridiculous was understood by none in her family since the death of her mother. They looked upon Georgette's placid exterior as her substance, never guessing the bubbling cauldron of devilry beneath. 'I hold,' said the reverend gentleman, 'that the exercise of dancing may become injurious to the health *and*, to the *morals* of the nation.' Georgette was sipping a negus cup in the throng around the supper table, and she answered, as his bulging eyes looked at her expectantly, 'Indeed sir, you think dancing *dangerous* to the body?'

'I see you are surprised, my dear Miss Fortune! I do not wonder at it. It is so *common* to think of dancing these days as *beneficial*. Indeed, parents employ dancing popinjays to teach their daughters. Then those same young ladies are encouraged to dance every dance and quite wear their feet away.'

'It is the feet, then, which you seek to protect?' said Georgette, still sipping the negus.

'Worse than the feet, I fear, are the temperate humours that keep the passions in check. These are vital to our health, yet let a man (or worse, a lady, I suggest) caper about a room for even an half-hour, and these have been so agitated that the very rules of civilisation may be ignored because such excitations have been allowed. Why, the English temperament becomes ever closer to the *Latin*.' Georgette's eyes widened in faux shock over her cup. 'We know how *they* conduct themselves. It is, in my idea, the product of the heat and being ill-bred.'

'I expect you warn your parishioners of the dangers,' remarked Georgette, enjoying herself shamefully, still sipping at her cup.

'I do. It may be that the upper classes might just possess the discipline of spirit to control themselves in a ballroom, but all country dances for the working man are to be discouraged. A young gentleman, but ten years ago, was taken ill after much dancing and when the surgeons opened him up there was seen to be *putrefaction* of the organs. Ah! I have shocked you, I fear. I might have spared your delicate ears such sad truths. But a warning I must give to those I regard.' Georgette gave a jolt to be included in this company, but stilled as he continued. 'I myself have felt the ill effects. It is not *natural* for a man to jump and shake his innards so! It was not thus decreed by the Almighty. You have observed that persons beyond the age of thirty restrict such posturing. With age comes wisdom, perhaps.'

Or exhaustion, thought Georgette. 'But I have met you at three balls already this season, Reverend Fullerton, and I do not believe *you* would seek to injure yourself.'

'You are very wise, my dear Miss Fortune, very wise. *I* dance, it is true. But here is the secret, my dear.' He bent forward, as though imparting one, but his voice was still booming. 'I do not dance to excess, *never* to excess.'

'It is true, Mr Fullerton,' said Georgette as though much struck. 'You danced perhaps three dances all evening, I have observed. When you did me the honour to dance with me this evening you did so with the most economy of movement. I remarked upon it. It was almost as though you were not dancing at all ...'

Then came the moment that changed her life. For over the shoulder of the vicar, and over the shoulder of a gentleman with his back to him, Georgette met the humorous eye of a tall, blond gentleman who seemed to have been listening for some time, perhaps. In that look, which caused the lines around sky-blue eyes to deepen, she saw his shared joy of the absurdity, and his knowledge of her own role in encouraging the display. The six feet between them seemed to retract as the look held, and she felt as though his whole being was closer to her than any gentleman had ever been, excepting her father and brother. But it was a simple illusion, neither of them had moved. She dimpled and blushed — then his attention was taken once more by his male companion. It was the work of but two seconds.

The Reverend Mr Fullerton continued to praise her for her observation and she hardly heard him. She had turned her face towards him once more and saw the fleshly lips move and bulging eyes search her face, but was only vaguely aware.

Someone had seen her, really seen her — and she was shaken to the core.

She was so aware of the tall gentleman that her peripheral vision grew larger. He moved away with his friend in the direction of the ballroom and she was able to notice a thatch of blond hair whose curls disobeyed pomade, whose tall frame was elegantly covered in a black coat and buff knee breeches, and whose large form carried away with it her heart.

This was the Lord Onslow that now, two years later, had not even recognised her.

to read on:
getbook.at/Georgette

Afterword

You might have noticed that an 'A' name crept into this book ... I wrote it for *Angelique and Other Stories*, only just finished it, and shall not apologise. I like the name Annis, and could not change it.

I added these stories to my novella *Euphemia and the Unexpected enchantment* only so that I might have the 'E' of my alphabetical titles. But it benefits my lovely readers, yourself included, since it is a free addition, requiring only a kindle update if you have read it before. I so enjoyed writing them and hope you like reading them.

They do not come out alphabetically, but will eventually make a satisfying shelf on my bookcase. (In case you haven't noticed they all have longer titles with the girl's name first, as in Angelique, Beth, Clarissa, Delphine, Euphemia, Felicity, Georgette, Honoria, Ianthe (pronounced eye an-thay, as so many people ask me.) Jocasta, Katerina, Leonora, Marguerite, Naomi...and now also Ursilla, since I have still to write the rest of the Wild Marchmont stories. Nothing is in series order, it is just a little joy of mine to aim for an alphabet.

Printed in Great Britain
by Amazon